Love's Road Home

Love's Road Home

Lisa Lewis

Black Lyon Publishing, LLC

Our books may be ordered through your local bookstore or by
visiting the publisher:

www.BlackLyonPublishing.com

Black Lyon Publishing, LLC
PO Box 567
Baker City, OR 97814

This is a work of fiction. All of the characters, names, events,
organizations and conversations in this novel are either the products
of the author's vivid imagination or are used in a fictitious way for the
purposes of this story.

ISBN-10:   1-934912-25-5
ISBN-13:   978-1-934912-25-6
Library of Congress Control Number: 2010921721

Written, published and printed in
the United States of America.

Black Lyon Contemporary Romance

For my family – Oscar, Tessa, and Bethany.
I hope this makes you proud.

For my parents - Emily and George.
I'm glad you liked the book Ma, and I'm sorry
Daddy never had the chance to read it.

Thanks to everyone who gave help and hope along the
way, especially Oscar and Sandy.

And special thanks to Chris of Albany's Palace Theatre,
who graciously shared his knowledge of concert tours with me.
Any variations from true roadie/band life are strictly
my own, for the sake of the story.

Chapter One

Tom Crowley's guitar fell silent, leaving only the echo of his last chords sounding in his band's makeshift rehearsal hall. Problem was, the song wasn't over yet.

"Hey, Tommy, what's goin' on? You don't like the song anymore?" Leo Harper grinned at Tom from his position at the lead microphone, his thick East Texas accent showing itself once again.

Tom shook his head, trying to get back on track. He just had to erase the image lingering in his mind. He'd only caught a glimpse of her, and he was sure no one could look that good up close. "Sorry, Leo. Let's take it from the top again, okay?"

Tom strummed the intro to their song "Dandelions," and listened as Leo began to croon the melody. Their band, Roadhouse, was launching an East Coast tour in two days in support of their recently recorded debut album. After singing at various clubs in and around their hometown of Savannah, they were finally moving things up a notch.

Just as Tom joined in, blending his baritone voice with Leo's in the song's chorus, he saw her again—the same vision of beauty that had disrupted him on the last run through. She was wandering around the room as if searching for someone. Luckily, he kept himself focused and made it through the whole song without embarrassing himself again.

"Okay, let's break for fifteen," Leo suggested. "We can't wear ourselves out before we play the first big gig."

The other band members left their instruments and moved toward the warehouse space that currently housed beer and snacks. But Tom set down his guitar and walked over to his friend. "Hey, Leo, who's that blonde over with George? I haven't seen her before."

George Miller was the road manager that the record producer had hired for their tour. Tom considered the band lucky to have him. He'd been in the business for thirty-odd years, and they were the greenhorns. The band was counting on George's expertise to get them through their first touring experience with as few problems as possible.

"That's George's daughter. She's going to be around for the tour, I guess."

"What do you mean, 'be around'?"

"George hired her as a roadie for us."

Tom couldn't hide the surprised look on his face. "What? Her? A roadie?"

"You got a problem with that, talk to George. We all knew he had carte blanche with hiring the tour crew."

"Yeah, I know we did, but what kind of work can she do? Is this just nepotism or what?"

Leo shrugged. "Hey, I trust George to know what has to be done and that all his crew members can pull their own weight. Like I said, you don't like it, talk to him. I gotta hit the john. See you in a few." Leo gave a jaunty salute and headed toward the bathroom.

Tom turned back toward the tall, leggy blonde, still engaged in conversation with her father. He truly thought she was a sight to behold, but good looks wouldn't keep their tour from being a disaster. And it was his professional life that needed attention, not his sex life.

He purposefully moved toward the couple, determined to get some answers.

•

"I told you, Dad, I can handle this. I won't let you down." Beth Miller was tired of repeating herself. If her father didn't trust her to do a good job, then he should have said so in the first place. Lord knew she couldn't sink any lower than she already had, and an early morning McDonald's shift surely would have taught her a lesson she deserved.

"Anything you want me to do, ask," she continued. "Don't do me any favors by trying to make this job easier. You already did more than you should've by hiring me as a roadie in the first place."

"Yes, Bethany, I hired you. But I'd also understand if you weren't

comfortable being back in this environment and had to leave."
George sighed. "I just don't need the hassle of finding a new roadie
in mid-tour. The boys are depending on me to keep everything
running smoothly."

The "boys" her father spoke of were really grown men who
acted like juveniles. Beth had no desire to be around such people,
but right now her options were limited. "I'm sure the boys would
understand if something happens. Every tour you've been on in
the last thirty-four years couldn't have gone perfectly. Things just
happen, right? And, besides, I told you there won't be any problems
caused by me. I promise."

"Hey, George, how are things shaping up? We going to be
heading out on schedule?"

Beth jumped as the whiskey-smooth voice spoke from behind
her, practically in her ear.

"Everything is fine, Tom." George waved a hand toward Beth
as a tall, masculine form moved to her left. "Have you met my
daughter, Bethany? She's going to be helping us out on the road."

Beth was stunned. She'd seen all the band members from a
distance while they practiced, but this was the first time she'd met
one of them up close. And this one was really close. She looked
into his dark brown eyes and felt the heat of his body even before
he stepped toward her, arm outstretched.

"Nice to make your acquaintance, Bethany. I'm Tom. Tom
Crowley." His handsome face lit up as he sent a crooked grin her
way. "But you probably knew that, right?"

Beth shook herself out of the mental fog she'd been in.
She'd already learned that good looks and good character were
independent traits, and she would not go down that road again.
Ignoring Tom's proffered hand, she sent him a disparaging look.
"No, actually I didn't. I'm not a fan of the band, and I'm not much
into country music in general."

The grin slid off Tom's face as he slowly lowered his arm. Her
father sent her a look of admonishment, but Beth didn't feel the
least ashamed of her words.

"Didn't you say the amps and speakers had to be inventoried
and marked before being loaded tomorrow? I'll go find Cole so we
can get started." Ignoring Tom and George's looks of disbelief, she
turned and marched off to find the fellow roadie.

•

"What the hell is her problem?" Even though the woman had completely irritated him, Tom couldn't help staring after her, noting the sexy sway of her hips as she stalked away.

"She's got so many of them right now, I wouldn't know where to begin."

Tom turned back to George, lifting an eyebrow in inquiry.

"Not that it'd be my business to tell you any of her problems anyway," George continued. "You can ask her yourself, if you dare."

Tom tucked that idea in the back of his mind, but then got back to the reason for interrupting the man's conversation in the first place.

"Look, George, I really just want to know if your daughter can handle herself. I mean, we need this tour to proceed on schedule, with as few screw-ups as possible. We need to have people around who can do the hard labor, move the heavy equipment. Your girl, Bethany, right?" He waited for George's nod. "She doesn't look capable of lifting fifty pounds let alone a couple hundred. And besides that, where's she going to stay? In all your years in the business, I bet you rarely came across a female among the roadies."

George waved his arms in a calming gesture. The older man's brown hair was thinning, but his otherwise toned body didn't reveal his age. "Now hold on there, Tom, it's all been figured out. First of all, Bethany might not look too strong, but she'll do whatever she needs to do. She's a tough cookie, inside and out. And second, she'll be bunking with Hannah and Liz while we're on the road. Marty already okayed all the hiring and travel arrangements. I checked with him as soon as I brought Bethany on board two days ago."

Tom felt a little more at ease knowing that Roadhouse's manager, Marty Sills, had approved the crew changes. And he knew the friendly back-up singers wouldn't mind sharing their living quarters with Bethany for the next five weeks. The more, the merrier, they would say.

"All right. Sorry, George, for being so worried, but we really need to show our stuff the next few weeks, and I guess the stress is getting to me. I'm sure everything will be fine." He gave the man a smile as he watched his band mates regrouping for additional rehearsal. "Talk to you later."

As Tom headed back toward his friends, his smile slipped away. For some reason, he had a feeling this tour wasn't going to be as untroubled as he'd hoped.

•

Beth dropped down onto the barstool and signaled to the man wiping down the oak countertop. "I'll have a light beer. Whatever you have on tap."

As the foamy brew was set down in front of her, Beth let out a long, deep breath and allowed the soft bluegrass tunes coming from the jukebox to wash over her. She was beat. She knew office work made people soft, but she'd thought her workouts at the company gym five times a week had kept her in decent shape. Was she ever wrong. She hadn't really known the meaning of sore muscles until today.

Now, after her first day of being a roadie, she was exhausted. Not only physically, but mentally. It had been hard work fighting the constant compulsion to watch Tom Crowley as he rehearsed. Ever since her encounter with him earlier in the day, she couldn't stop thinking about him. Beth knew she'd been rude, but it was pretty much how she was with everyone lately. He'd merely been unfortunate enough to be in the wrong place at the wrong time and ended up suffering from her caustic tongue.

She felt a lot better now.

Her father had risked a lot by hiring her to work on Roadhouse's premiere tour, and Beth knew she owed him for that. It had taken her a couple weeks of feeling sorry for herself before she'd called George and asked for his help. Just in time, too, because her savings account was nearly empty.

Taking a long draw of her beer, Beth looked around the dimly lit club. It was pretty empty, but that was to be expected at three o'clock on a Thursday afternoon. This place probably didn't see much action until the weekend, when local bands played to a full house of dancing, flirting, party-hardy people. Beth idly wondered if Roadhouse had ever played here.

Which brought her thoughts right back to Tom Crowley.

She'd never seen a sexier man. He wasn't attractive in a big-city, polished sort of way, but in a laid-back aw-shucks ma'am manner. She had never been attracted to men like that before, but something about this man had captured her attention. It could've been the deep chocolate-brown eyes that had twinkled at her, or the wicked grin he'd tossed her way. She'd absolutely loved how his dark hair was styled, trimmed fairly close to his scalp yet still long enough for a woman to run her fingers through it. Really hot. And Beth definitely knew that his voice had captivated her with its smooth southern drawl.

Too bad he hadn't had something interesting to say with that voice.

Oh, well.

Beth smiled to herself and took another swig of beer. At least she had a job now and could feel proud of herself for doing hard, honest work.

"That smile for any reason in particular?"

She nearly choked on her beer. Her thoughts must have conjured him up because Tom Crowley was standing just behind her right shoulder. Coughing and trying to catch her breath, she couldn't resist giving him the once-over. Still dressed in the worn jeans and gray T-shirt he'd had on earlier, Tom looked cool and relaxed. She, on the other hand, felt haggard and grubby in her own shirt and jeans, having come straight to the bar from work. She hadn't expected to socialize with anyone, least of all Tom.

"Sorry. I didn't mean to startle you." Tom gestured to the empty stool beside her. "Do you mind if I sit?"

Cautiously, Beth shook her head. She wondered what he wanted.

"I wasn't sure if you'd be here or not. Your father said you were going to get a drink, and I took a chance that you headed here to Gregory's, seeing as it was the closest bar."

Surprised, she asked, "You were looking for me?"

"Yeah. I thought we got off on the wrong foot, and I didn't want to spend the next month on the road avoiding each other for a no-good reason. I wanted to start over again, with no assumptions being made. Fair enough?"

Beth slowly took a drink of beer, pondering his words and the real reason behind them. Maybe it was the alcohol, or maybe it was her improved mood after a difficult day's work was over. Regardless, she decided to give him a chance.

"Fair enough."

◆

Tom slowly let out the breath he'd been unconsciously holding. He wasn't sure what exactly had driven him to seek out this prickly woman, but now that he'd found her, he really did want to start over. For the sake of the tour, he reminded himself. Not for personal reasons.

He extended his hand. "Hi. My name's Tom Crowley. I sing and play lead guitar for Roadhouse. I hear you're going to be working with us on our tour."

A slender, lightly tanned hand slipped into his, giving a strong, firm shake before withdrawing. "Nice to meet you, Tom. I'm Beth Miller."

Tom got the bartender's attention and gave an order for whiskey on the rocks. Then he turned back to his companion. "Your father called you Bethany earlier. You don't like that?"

She scrunched up her nose and shrugged. "It's fine, I guess. It just makes me feel like a little girl again when he calls me that. But I suppose it's better than what he says when I disappoint him. 'Oh, Bethie. What have you done now?' I can still hear those words in my head whenever I do something wrong."

"Well, I think Bethany is a real classy name. Although Beth is cool, too. Did you ever hear the Kiss ballad called "Beth?" It's a great song."

He sang softly, "Beth, I hear you callin' ..."

Beth smiled and rolled her eyes at him. "Are you kidding? Of course I've heard it. In fact, I was named after that song. My parents made out endlessly to seventies music, and I might even have been conceived to it. Not that I like to think about stuff like that." Beth shuddered dramatically at the thought.

Tom chuckled and took a swallow of his drink. "Yeah, no one likes to think about their parents doing it." And he was trying really hard not to think about himself doing it ... with Bethany. "Did George ever roadie for Kiss? He was on the road during their heyday, right?"

A shadow crossed over Beth's face but quickly disappeared. "I don't think he worked with them, although he's been traveling with different bands longer than I've been alive. Rock and roll, grunge, rap, and now country acts. He's done it all, and he never seems to tire of it. I sometimes think he'll die on the road, hauling equipment for one band or another." She took another sip of her beer.

"Would that bother you, if he went that way? I mean, if he's doing what he loves when he goes, would that be so bad? Not that he's going to die any time soon, in my opinion. He looks healthy as a horse, in great shape for his age. Do you know anything different?"

Beth glared at him over her glass, her light blue eyes shining like icicles. "Don't worry. To my knowledge, nothing is going to ruin your precious tour. Least of all the death of my father."

Tom glared right back at her, offended by what she was thinking. "Okay, listen here. I was trying to make conversation with you. Trying to find out more about you, maybe. But I was not, under any circumstances, trying to ensure my own career status by pulling some inside information from you. Nothing was further from my mind. I consider George a friend, not just a co-worker, and I asked about his health in that capacity. Contrary to whatever you believe, I do care about people other than myself."

Beth ducked her head, shielding her face behind a curtain of long blonde hair. "I'm sorry. I've been in a real bad mood today, and you always seem to be the one I take it out on. I guess I've just been inclined to think the worst about everyone I meet lately. I'm real sorry."

She tucked her hair behind one ear and looked at him with a small, hopeful smile on her face. "Please, can we start over again? Like you said, it'll be a long five weeks if we can't act civil to each other."

Studying Bethany's face, Tom tried once again to not think about being more than civil to each other. A slightly upturned nose. High cheekbones and expressive silvery-blue eyes. Full lips and smooth, sun-kissed skin. Nice features individually, but together they formed a picture of true beauty. He really wanted to get to know this woman better.

"All right. But this is your last chance. You can only push my restart button a couple of times before I completely shut down." Tom gave her a quick smile to soften his words, letting her know he was kidding. After taking another sip of whiskey, he asked, "But really, how was your first day as a roadie? Things go okay?"

Beth nodded. "Yeah. We loaded up as much as we could on the truck today, and we're going to finish up tomorrow after the band's final rehearsal. Cole, Mike, and the other guys were really helpful.

They showed me what to do and didn't yell too much if I messed up."

"You'll get the hang of it. The crew seems like a good group, and we really are glad your father took the job as road manager. I think Freestone Records did the right thing in asking him to work with us. With his help, and the way the tour schedule has been planned out, we're thinking things will run pretty smooth."

"I haven't had time to check out the exact tour itinerary." Beth leaned an elbow on the bar and propped her cheek against her curled hand. "We're hitting some major cities on the East Coast, right?"

"Major cities, minor cities, and everywhere in between. Basically, this is Roadhouse's trial run in the limelight. If we can't fill the seats, there's no sense in planning any more tour dates after this trip. And Marty, our manager, arranged a very specific route, too."

"What do you mean?"

"Marty is big with building anticipation. He wants to draw in as many fans and ticket buyers as he can along the way. What better way to do that than through local media coverage and word of mouth?"

Bethany still looked puzzled so Tom continued on. "It's like this. Our first show is in Jacksonville—only a hundred and fifty miles away yet it's far enough to be a pain when getting the equipment moved. But when the reviews of our performance hit the TV and newspapers, Jacksonville is close enough so people here in the Savannah area might catch some of them. Assuming we do a good job and the talk is good, our next show in Macon will have gained some additional concertgoers."

"But you guys have been playing around here for years. Wouldn't anybody who'd wanted to see you perform done so by now? And all it would have cost them would've been a cover charge for the bar entry. Why would anybody be foolish enough to shell out an indecent amount of money to see a less intimate show in a big auditorium?" A stricken look came across Beth's face, and she covered her mouth with her hand. "Please don't be offended. That really was just an innocent question, not a personal attack."

Tom let a soft laugh escape. "Don't worry. I'm beginning to see how you are. Speak first, think later. But in answer to your question, everyone who might've wanted to see Roadhouse perform wasn't able to before. Not all country music fans are gray-haired old ladies, you know. We're attracting listeners of all ages, some who've even crossed over from the rock or pop scene. Actually, the first time that 'Dandelions' was played on the radio it was on a Top 40 station, not a country one."

"So this tour really is an opportunity for all your fans to see you."

"Definitely. And since these shows will be a lot more extravagant than anything we've done in the local clubs, even the fans who've seen us before won't get the same old thing. The sound, the lighting, the whole atmosphere will be different in these larger venues." Tom rubbed his hands over his face and shook his head. "I get nervous just thinking about singing to a crowd of more than a few hundred people. This really is going to be a big step up for Roadhouse if we can pull it off."

"I'm sure you'll be great." Bethany lifted her half-empty glass of beer. "Here's to a successful tour. May you enjoy every second of your celebrity."

"Let's not rush things. Let's take it one day at a time." Tom lifted his own drink. "To Jacksonville," he said, and touched his glass to Beth's.

She smiled. "To Jacksonville."

·

In a stone mansion on the edge of Savannah's Historic District, a young woman ran up the stairs to her west wing bedroom. She was ecstatic, barely able to contain her excitement.

Pulling up the candid photos she'd loaded onto her PC, she sat down in front of the machine and let out a long sigh. It seemed like each passing minute was an hour.

But soon she'd see him on stage. Live and in person.

She'd been waiting for this moment for a long time. Okay, a year—but it had seemed like forever. And now she didn't have to wait much longer to meet him.

He was going to be in a public arena. A huge theatre. She didn't have to worry about getting a fake ID in order to gain access to a local bar. There was no age limit for admittance to the upcoming concert, and she was going to be there. Not quite in the front row, but close enough that he would see her while he played.

She was so proud of him. He was on his way to the big time now, and she intended to be by his side as he finally got all the recognition he deserved. He was so gorgeous and talented. And he was hers.

At least he would be, once they finally met face to face.

Chapter Two

Beth put down her bottle of lemonade and looked around. The stage was all set for Roadhouse's performance later that evening, and the crew of roadies and local stagehands were taking a well-deserved break.

Her job had been decided right after she'd been hired. Laying electrical wires meant less heavy lifting for her to do, and it freed other guys for jobs she couldn't necessarily do as a rookie. Or as a woman. As the final equipment was being broken down and packed up in Savannah yesterday afternoon, Mike had given her a brief rundown on how the lines had to be arranged and connected.

Beth had traveled down to Jacksonville in the same van as her father and Cole. Although she was quick to pick up new skills, she had to admit that the onslaught of electrical terminology Mike had thrown at her earlier had been a bit overwhelming. She'd been glad to have the opportunity in the truck to ask the two men a few additional questions.

Upon their arrival in the area early this morning, the crew had proceeded to check out the accommodations in the Florida Theatre. They needed to verify where all the equipment was to be arranged, where the stage exits and dressing rooms were, and other technical information that could change from one venue to another. Beth had enjoyed taking part in those activities, which added to her understanding of the many aspects of a roadie's job. Once the initial inspection had been completed, everyone got right to work on the load-in and set-up of equipment.

Now, as she looked at the job she'd just completed, Beth was satisfied. Mike was still going to look over her wiring connections to be sure they were correct, but she thought they'd be fine. Her confidence was high even though her hands-on experience was low. And once she mastered this part of her job, hopefully more duties would be assigned to her.

Because Beth was really hoping that additional work would keep her mind off Tom Crowley.

The other night in Savannah, at Gregory's bar, she had really enjoyed talking with Tom. Maybe too much. He'd treated her with respect and spoke in a very cordial manner, yet subtle glances he'd sent her way had conveyed his attraction to her. And Beth was sure he'd probably gotten the same vibe from her all evening, no matter how much she'd tried to hide it.

She really didn't want to encourage attention from a man like Tom. Now, or any time soon. Things in her life were just too complicated at the moment, and she wasn't sure when, or if, they were going to be straightened out.

After polishing off her lemonade, Beth whistled and waved her arms at Mike, currently at stage left hooking up the keyboards. "Hey, Mike, you want to check out my work when you get a chance?"

"Be right there," he yelled back to her. He spoke briefly to the roadie who was assembling the drum set, then jumped off the stage and headed toward Beth at the mixing board.

•

Tom tried to be subtle as he looked around the theatre, searching for Beth among the various crew members doing equipment checks. The band didn't need to start their last run-through of songs for a few more hours, and it was near lunchtime now. He was hoping he could talk Bethany into joining him for a bite to eat.

He finally caught sight of her near the center of the auditorium, speaking with another technician. Tom headed her way, admiring the way she looked even in casual work clothes of T-shirt and jeans. Her blonde hair was pulled back in a ponytail, allowing him a clear view of her profile.

As Tom approached the pair, Mike threw him a wave. "Hey, Tom. Things are shaping up fine for tonight. Beth is going to do terrific on the tour, I can tell already." With a nod, he began moving back toward the stage. "See you later."

The look on Beth's face wasn't nearly as welcoming as Mike's greeting had been.

What, did she think he was going to jump her bones right this moment? As his eyes traveled over her body, Tom knew he definitely would have no problem doing that. But he also knew if he seriously wanted to get closer to Beth, he had to move slowly.

"Hi, Beth. How's the job going?"

She seemed to relax a bit in reaction to his business-like question. "So far, so good. Mike only needed to make two minor adjustments in my wiring layout. He said it was great work for a novice."

"That's good. But we'll find out later if everything's hooked up right."

"Yeah, I guess so." Beth flashed a brief smile.

"You know, it looks like you're all done for now, and we don't have to be back here for sound check for at least a couple of hours. Do you want to grab some lunch?"

She looked surprised at his offer. Then she quickly shook her head no. "I really can't. I'm sure the crew has more work to do. At the very least, Mike will want me to stick around and observe."

Just then Mike announced via the lead microphone, "Lunch break, everyone. Be back here by four o'clock sharp for sound check."

Tom grinned at Beth. "Any other excuse you want to use?"

She frowned back at him. "Well, actually I'm not dressed properly. And I'm sweaty and dirty from working, too."

"You're dressed fine. It's not like we're going to a four-star restaurant. Just hit the bathroom to wash the grime off your hands and face and we'll head out."

Beth looked appalled. "I have something on my face? How bad is it?"

Tom reached toward her. "It's just a small bit of dirt. Don't panic." Gently he smoothed his fingers over her soft cheek, brushing off the minute soil particles that contrasted with her lighter complexion. The instant his flesh touched hers he felt a connection. An electric current that swept through his entire being.

Slowly he lowered his hand, wondering if she'd felt it, too. "Come on," he coaxed softly. "Come with me."

"All right."

♦

Beth pretended interest in the passing scenery as Tom drove a black Ford SUV through the Jacksonville streets. "So, where did you say we were going?"

"We have enough time before sound check to hit the beach. It's only half an hour away. I figured we could grab some seafood and take a quick walk on the sand. Sound good to you?"

It sounded dangerous, actually. She couldn't believe she'd agreed to go out with him. But Beth turned to Tom and said, "Sounds great." She watched as he confidently maneuvered the city streets. "You seem pretty familiar with the area around here. Have you visited Jacksonville a lot? You told me the other night that you were born and raised in Savannah."

Tom smiled. "Yeah, I'm a Savannah boy through and through, but I did leave to attend college. University of North Florida, right here in Jacksonville. Leo and I shared an off-campus apartment, and we got to know the area well when we played different gigs."

"Gigs?" She thought some of the music terms he used were cute. "You mean Roadhouse has been performing for what, ten years, and you guys are only hitting it big now?"

He stopped at a flashing red light and turned to give her a quizzical look. "Didn't you get any information about the band from your father when he hired you?"

She shook her head.

As they continued down the road, Tom explained, "Leo's family moved to Savannah when we were both freshmen, and we've been best friends ever since. Each of us loved music, was in the school band, and dreamed about becoming a famous rock star. After graduation, we both decided to go to the university in Jacksonville. We didn't hook up with the rest of Roadhouse until after college, about five years ago."

Digesting this piece of Tom's history, Beth asked, "Okay, so what kind of gigs did you and Leo do in college? Frat parties? Bar Mitzvahs? Weddings?"

"Basically, anyone who paid us to sing, we'd do it. But since we ultimately decided we weren't interested in the hard rock, headbanger music scene, we mostly played tamer, upscale kinds of parties. We had kind of a Simon and Garfunkel thing going. We both played saxophone in high school, but I really wasn't great at it. I taught myself guitar and discovered I was better off using my mouth for singing."

Beth slanted a quick glance at his sensual lips and figured he had mastered plenty of skills involving that body part. Of course, his hands looked mighty fine, too. Strong but lean, with long fingers and neatly trimmed nails. She pulled her gaze back to the city streets, trying to refocus on the conversation. "Did you write your own songs in college?"

"At first we covered a lot of other bands, just to build a name for ourselves in the area. Over time, we started to insert some of our own work into the sets, and the songs were well received. Actually, 'Dandelions' is a tune that I began to write back in college. I finished it last year, we put it on the album, and it was released as the first single."

Tom swung the vehicle into a public lot near the beach and parked. He got out and came around to Beth's side, opening her door before she could do it. Holding out a hand, he asked, "Are you ready?"

She honestly didn't think she'd ever be ready for a man like Tom.

◆

Tom waited as Beth hesitantly extended her hand. He understood why she'd be afraid, after their earlier connection. He still wondered if it had really happened. Now, as she placed her hand into his, he felt it again. She looked up, showing him with her widened, silver-blue eyes that he wasn't alone in the feeling.

He tugged on her arm, gently pulling her out of the truck and closer to him. He didn't back up but instead trapped her between his body and the truck door. Still holding her hand, caught in her beautiful gaze, he asked, "How hungry are you? Because, right now, I'm starving."

He watched as she caught his double-entendre and a faint blush rose up her cheeks. But she didn't back down from his less-than-subtle advance. Instead, she gave a mysterious little smile and replied, "I think I'm getting hungrier by the minute. It must be catching."

Tom raised his other hand to cup her cheek, caressing her jaw line with his thumb. Her mouth dropped open in an invitation he couldn't resist. He slowly lowered his head toward Beth's, giving her ample opportunity to back away. He'd been imagining this kiss from the first moment he'd seen her only a couple of days ago.

"Hey, buddy! You leaving or what?"

Tom jumped away from Beth, startled by the shout and honking horn of an impatient driver. Apparently he wanted their parking space, like right now.

"Sorry, guy, but we just got here." The man gave an angry little gesture and inched his car down the aisle, searching for an available spot.

Tom turned back to Beth, knowing that he'd missed his opportunity. The mood was broken, and from the way she was looking everywhere but at him, it definitely wasn't coming back anytime soon.

Again catching her hand in his, he said, "Come on. Let's go eat the best haddock on the East Coast."

He locked up the truck with the click of a button, and they headed off down the boardwalk.

•

"This place is great," Beth said. She looked at the fishing equipment decorating the walls of the diner and laughed. "Who knew that fishing poles could double as curtain rods?" She slid into the booth indicated by the hostess and Tom took a seat opposite her. Colorful menus were placed in front of them.

"Yeah, Fred went a touch overboard with the maritime theme, but I guess he wanted to be sure people didn't try to order steak."

"Fred? You know the owner personally?"

"Fred and I took business courses together in college. We've kept in touch over the years, and Roadhouse has performed for some of his beach parties out back."

Beth was confused. "I thought you studied music in college. Was I wrong in assuming that? From what you said before, it seemed like a career in music is all you've ever wanted since high school."

"It's all I've ever wanted, but my family didn't necessarily share my goals."

A waitress came to get their order, and after quickly scanning the menus, they decided upon fish frys, onion rings, and sodas. The woman collected the menus and moved off to the kitchen.

Resuming their discussion, Beth asked, "What do you mean by that?"

Tom gave a wry smile. "It's hard to make it in the music business, and my family wanted to make sure I was prepared for failure."

"That's horrible! They didn't think you had the talent to succeed?"

"No, that's not it at all. My parents were very supportive of my career choice, and they thought I had plenty of talent. But a lot of this business depends on who you know and good old-fashioned luck. Being in the right place at the right time. My parents wanted me to have a back-up plan in case good things didn't happen for me music-wise." He shrugged. "I haven't had a problem with that."

"So what did you do?"

"My father owns a hardware store in Savannah. It's been in the family for three generations. We agreed that I would minor in business at college in preparation for taking over the store and continuing the family business."

"And you were okay with that?"

"Hey, the hardware store's been good to me. I've been working there part-time to help pay the bills the last few years. And it's not like my father is pressuring me to run the business right away. Like I said, he's very supportive of my music, and he knows I have to do this now, while Roadhouse really has a chance at making it big. He knows in the end that I'll always come back home."

Beth suppressed a sigh. It must be nice to have such a reliable home life. She wasn't even sure what home was anymore.

"What about your mother? Is she as happy for you?"

Tom's features immediately softened. "My mom died four years ago. Cancer. She didn't get a chance to see Roadhouse's success, but I'm sure she would've been happy to see our progress over the years. She didn't like the instability of a career in music, didn't think it was conducive to supporting a family."

How true she knew that to be. Beth felt a twinge in her heart at Tom's words, but she ignored it. This was not about her.

"But Mom stuck by all my choices and suffered silently while her little boy chased his dreams." Tom smiled with a bit of melancholy. "I miss her."

She wasn't sure how to respond to his comments, so Beth remained silent. The lull in conversation was interrupted by the arrival of their food, and the discussion soon turned to generic topics like the tour, the weather, and seafood.

As they finished the last of their meal, Tom glanced at his wristwatch. "We need to head out in order to get back to the theatre by four. I guess we talked too much and ate too slow."

He refused her offer of going Dutch for the meal, stating that he'd asked her out so he was paying. As they stood at the register, Beth looked at Tom, thinking once again what a decent guy he was. The fact that he was gorgeous was just a bonus. She decided she wouldn't mind spending more time with him as the tour progressed. As a friend, of course. That's all.

He held the door for her as they left the diner and started back toward the parked truck. "What's that look for?"

Beth glanced up at him but kept walking. "What look?"

"You looked like you were stuck between a rock and a hard place."

"No, not exactly." More like she had to choose between what her head wanted and what her heart wanted.

"So what is it then?"

She stopped at the front of the SUV, turned to face him. Better to get this out of the way now. "It's about what happened earlier. Or rather, what almost happened."

A small masculine smile curved his lips upward. "You mean when we almost kissed?"

"Yes, that's what I mean. It can't happen again."

The smile instantly disappeared. "Why the hell not? It looked to me like you were enjoying our little flirtation, and I know I certainly was. What's so different now?"

"Nothing is different. I just lost my head earlier. I don't know what I was thinking, or if I was thinking at all. I'm sorry, but I have too many things up in the air right now, and I need to straighten out my life. I really can't get involved with you at this point."

As she turned to move toward the passenger door, Tom took hold of her arm, stopping her retreat. She looked at him again, noting the hard glint of determination in his brown eyes.

"Sorry to break this to you, honey, but it's too late. We're already involved."

•

The drive back to the Florida Theatre was made in silence. Evidently Beth didn't agree with his statement about their relationship, but Tom wasn't concerned. They had plenty of time to interact during the next few weeks on tour. He'd slowly but surely break through whatever wall she was hiding behind. He knew having her would be worth the time and effort.

The rest of the night passed in a flurry of activity. They had sound check and a final rehearsal of particular songs. The set list and lighting arrangements were verified. Wardrobe and instruments were inspected for the last time. Everything appeared to be in order for Roadhouse's tour debut.

Tom saw Beth here and there in the auditorium, but he didn't speak to her. He was too focused on making this concert the best performance of his life. His future, and that of his band mates, depended upon tonight. He wasn't going to let anything, or anyone, distract him.

Finally it was time to go on. They had no opening band for the tour since they wanted all the attention on themselves. Roadhouse had prepared a set list for a two-hour performance, leaving a twenty-minute intermission after the first hour. With only one free night scheduled per week, the band needed to address any flaws in their performance during rehearsals. On stage, they needed to shine.

The pounding of Tom's heart almost drowned out the audience's welcoming applause once the band took the stage. He had never seen such a mass of people, all there to listen to his music. Leo immediately signaled for the start of their first number, a tune guaranteed to get the crowd on its feet. And Roadhouse didn't intend for them to ever sit down again.

The adrenaline was still coursing through Tom's veins two and a half hours later. He couldn't believe how great everything had gone. The equipment had all worked perfectly, and not a single note was missed in any song, vocally or instrumentally. The audience had clapped and cheered for multiple encores, but Roadhouse had to finally leave the stage for good because it was getting too late. He felt on top of the world, and the night wasn't over yet.

George had arranged for an area to be cordoned off for an autograph session. The band members sat at a long table and fans were directed to form a line to have their programs, CDs, and T-shirts signed. Tom wasn't sure exactly how well this segment of the night was going to go, but he was willing to give it a try. They could always ditch this aspect of the tour if they didn't draw a big enough crowd.

But it appeared he'd worried for nothing. Once again, he was stunned by the praise and excitement of the many concertgoers who had waited their turn to meet the band. As the half-hour autograph session was drawing to a close, there were still quite a few people left in line. A couple crew members were trying to move the fans along because, even though tomorrow was their day off, they still needed to get things closed up for the night.

Tom returned his gaze to the dark-haired young lady in front of him. She looked to be in her late teens or early twenties. "Who should I make this out to?" He smiled up at her, still feeling the energy of the evening.

"It's Casey, with a C." She sent a bright smile back his way.

"Did you enjoy the show, Casey with a C?" Tom wrote a brief message and signed his name across the program she'd set in front of him.

"Oh, yes. It was terrific. I especially love how you and Leo harmonize. Your voice is the greatest, and you play guitar so awesomely." As he watched, the girl's cheeks slowly began to burn.

"Well, thanks for coming tonight, Casey, and thanks for the compliments. I hope you continue to enjoy our music in the future."

"Oh, I know I will."

As Tom turned to the next person in line, a middle-aged woman who reminded him of his late mother, he didn't notice the fanatical gleam in the brunette's eyes as she slowly moved away.

Chapter Three

Macon was a beautiful little place compared to the sprawling metropolis of Jacksonville. It seemed like a nice town to spend a day off in, and, oddly enough—after only one show—today was it. Beth wasn't going to argue with the illogical concert schedule, but she was too tired to truly enjoy her respite. After eight hours of equipment load-out in Jacksonville followed by a two hundred and seventy mile trip, all she wanted now was a simple meal and a good night's sleep.

She'd spent most of the afternoon visiting local shops with Hannah and Liz, and that activity had pretty much exhausted her last energy reserves. The other women had just left with some of the roadies, heading out to dinner and then dancing. Beth had declined their invitation to go along, knowing she didn't have much time left before she fell flat on her face.

She hunted through the cupboards for anything that would stop her stomach from growling long enough for her to fall asleep, and, thankfully, her eyes landed on a package of snack crackers. They'd be perfect with the sliced cheese she'd seen in the mini fridge. A knock on the door stalled her movements just as she latched onto the box.

Still holding the crackers, Beth made her way to the motor home entrance. "Coming!" she yelled as she opened the box and grabbed a couple of squares. Popping the crackers into her mouth, she opened the door and froze, mid-chew.

"Hi, Beth." Tom greeted her with another one of his terrific smiles. The kind that made her breath catch in her throat. "I know it's been a long, hectic day, but I wanted to stop by and see if you had plans for tonight."

Beth quickly swallowed the remaining crackers in her mouth,

knowing she'd stood there staring at him like an idiot while he'd talked. He looked handsome and refreshed in a white polo shirt and khakis while she felt like the walking dead. Of course, he hadn't stayed up till the wee hours disassembling and reloading equipment, either. That must be why his warm, inviting eyes had no bags under them.

"You're looking at them."

He cocked an eyebrow upward. "Huh?"

She wiggled the box of crackers at him. "My plans for tonight. Cheese and crackers and then beddie-bye. I'm beat."

"Oh, now I can't allow that to happen. It's only five o'clock on a Sunday night, way too early to be pooped. Besides, you need more sustenance than cheese and crackers if you're going to set up for the concert tomorrow. Let me take you out for some real food."

Beth tilted her head to the side and asked, "How come you're always trying to feed me? Do I look too skinny to you?" She wanted to take back the question as soon as the words were out of her mouth. But it was too late. Tom's eyes slowly made their way down and then back up her body. She felt naked beneath his intense gaze, even in her shorts and T-shirt.

"You look terrific to me. Just the right size in all the right places." His low, sexy drawl and ardent stare captured her, holding her in place for a long moment. Then he casually shrugged, breaking the mood. "But really, I just wanted to spend more time with you, and it seems like the only thing there is to do on tour besides work is eat. And sleep, of course. But I couldn't invite you to do that with me."

"Yet," was his unspoken implication. But Beth let Tom's comment slide by without taking the bait. "If I do agree to have dinner with you, then it's only dinner, nothing else. And you have to promise that we'll be back in a couple hours. I really am bushed."

"I promise I won't make you do anything you don't want to. How's that?"

"Good enough, I suppose."

"Great. Now go get ready. I'll be back in thirty minutes to get you and then we're off to get a big, juicy steak."

•

Tom opened the SUV's passenger door so Beth could step up. He watched as she swung her legs into position, admiring the sleek, toned shape of them beneath the short skirt of her navy blue sundress. He was a sucker for killer legs on a female. Of course, on Beth, all her body parts were outstanding.

Closing the door while she buckled in, Tom moved around to the driver's side and took his place behind the wheel. Once they headed out of the parking lot, Beth asked, "How come you're always driving this SUV? Is it yours?"

"No. Marty rented it for the whole band and crew to use along the tour. He figured we'd get sick of being cooped up in the RVs during our down time, and we might want to get away for a while."

"But you seem to be the only one using it."

"There's a sign-up sheet in our trailer. Whoever wants to use the truck can sign it out ahead of time. Turns out no one but me has wanted it so far."

"A bunch of the guys went out tonight, and Hannah and Liz went with them."

"Yeah, I talked to them earlier. They're just headed to some clubs in walking distance of the auditorium. If they plan to have a few drinks then they made the right choice in hoofing it. And a taxi won't cost them too much if it turns out they really need one later."

"So we're going more than a few blocks away? Remember, I don't want to be out that long," Beth cautioned.

"Yes, Cinderella, you'll be home before the coach turns back into a pumpkin," Tom agreed in a resigned tone. He knew he'd change her mind before dinner was over. Because of last night's consecutive performance and traveling, they hadn't seen much of each other since their lunch together. This suited Tom's purposes fine, because he wanted to let Beth think he was backing off. She'd been so skittish at the beach yesterday, determined to avoid any kind of relationship with him.

They soon arrived at a steak house near the river, and the hostess escorted them to a candlelit table overlooking the Ocmulgee. Tom pulled out a chair for Beth, leaning close to breathe in the subtle fruity remnants of her quick shower. He took his time pushing her chair back into place before taking a seat opposite her. A companionable silence surrounded them while they perused the menus.

"Would you like some wine?" he asked.

Beth glanced up and shook her head. "No thanks. It would only make me more tired than I already am. But you can go ahead and order it if you want some."

"No, I'm fine with a tall glass of milk."

"Milk?" The incredulous look on Beth's face conveyed her disbelief.

"Of course," Tom insisted. "Salad, meat, and potatoes was the standard dinner in my household growing up, with a cold glass of milk to wash it all down. It does a body good, you know." He grinned, wondering how she'd respond to his last comment.

"You must've drunk gallons of it, then," she mumbled beneath her breath.

"What was that?" he asked innocently.

"Nothing. I'm just deciding what I want for dinner," Beth lied.

"Okay." Tom let the fib pass since he already knew Beth was as attracted to him as he was to her. His problem was getting her to admit it.

The waitress returned to collect their menus and take their dinner orders. Just as he'd said he would, Tom ordered a large milk along with his prime rib and baked potato. Beth ordered a steak and shrimp combo plate and a diet soda. Tom returned his gaze to Bethany's face as they were left alone once again, intent on discovering more about her.

"So. Tell me something about yourself. You learned quite a bit about me from our conversations, but I still know next to nothing about you. What was your childhood like? What's your favorite color? Your favorite ice cream flavor? Come on," Tom cajoled. "Give me something to work with."

Beth lifted her water glass and took a sip. Then she replied with a small smile, "Forest green and chocolate. How about you?"

"Light blue, like your eyes, and strawberry. But don't try to turn it back to me. What're your favorite movie and book?"

They spent the rest of dinner trading innocuous tidbits of information. Having noticed right away how Beth ignored his question about her childhood, Tom decided not to ruin the mood by pressing the issue. He was interested in any information she wanted to disclose about herself, but he wasn't going to truly understand her without more in-depth sharing ... and it appeared that would have to wait for a later time.

•

By the time they were finishing their coffee and pecan pie, Beth felt better. The lethargy that had consumed her earlier seemed to have dissipated. Tom's presence always energized her, which raised concern. She didn't want to feel anything special when she was around him. She just wanted to do her job and get through each day as peacefully as possible.

Beth knew Tom was curious about her. He had tried various times during dinner to draw her into a more intimate conversation, but she'd always backed off, keeping to general topics. It's not that she was trying to be mysterious or tease him in any way. She simply wanted to avoid discussing any painful and humiliating incidents in her life. And there seemed to be too many of them, especially recently.

"So. Be honest. Do you really want to go back to the RV now? Or do you want to check out some of the local scene?" Tom's smooth voice interrupted her thoughts and drew her gaze back to his face. He hadn't shaved since that morning, and his five-o'clock shadow served to accentuate the handsome masculine features beneath. The soft candlelight reflected in his deep brown eyes as he awaited her answer.

"Well, I hate to admit it since you seem awfully sure of yourself, but I wouldn't mind going out for a while. Nothing too physical, though. I have muscle aches in places I'd never dreamed. Maybe a short walk along the riverbank?"

"I have a better idea. Something more fun."

Beth narrowed her eyes and asked, "This does involve staying in a public place, right?"

Tom made a tsking noise, shaking his head. "A little suspicious, are we? Have no fear, sweetheart. I will always be a perfect gentleman around you. Unless you prefer otherwise?" he asked hopefully.

Beth rolled her eyes and shoved her chair back to stand up. "Come on, lover boy. Let's go."

Once again Tom paid the check, reinforcing the idea that this was an actual date. They returned to the truck and headed away from the restaurant.

"That was an excellent dinner. The food and service were both great. Thanks for suggesting it, and for taking me." As they drove down the road, Beth glanced at the variety of local businesses. "How did you know about that restaurant? Or did you just pick the first one in the phone book that had the word 'steak' in its name?"

"Actually, Mike told me about it."

"Mike, my fellow roadie?"

"Yeah. He's originally from Macon. I saw him earlier and asked if he could recommend a nice place for dinner in the area. He also told me about the place we're going to next."

Beth was silent a moment. "You planned ahead of time that we were going to dinner?"

"Well, I knew I was going to ask you. I wasn't exactly sure you would say yes. But I was hoping."

"What if I'd said no to you?"

"Well then, I guess I would've just skulked off to my bunk and cried myself to sleep." Tom turned to give her a pouty look. "And I would have starved because I know there's no cheese and crackers in my cupboards."

Beth laughed. "You are such a goofball."

He shot her a wide grin and merged into the next lane of traffic.

Then Beth was struck by a new thought. "You didn't mention my name to Mike, did you? I mean, you didn't tell him you were specifically going to ask me to dinner, right?"

"Yeah, I did. Why?"

She pressed a hand to her temple and closed her eyes, horrified. "Why did you do that? Oh, my God."

"What's the problem now?"

"Everyone on the tour is going to think we're dating. I really didn't want to give people that impression."

Tom turned the Ford into a large parking lot. The area was well lit and fairly crowded. A huge neon sign announced their arrival at the Megaplex of Fun. After finding an empty space and switching off the engine, Tom turned to Beth with an exasperated look on his face. "Look, the only one I spoke to was Mike. I didn't shout my intentions to the whole entourage, and who cares if people find out about tonight anyway? We are on a date, whether you want to admit it or not. Let's have some fun for an hour or so and not worry about the gossip that tomorrow might bring. Remember what I said in Savannah? About taking one day at a time? Well that applies to the tour and to us. Let's just see what happens tonight."

He didn't wait for a reply. Instead he just exited the truck and stood near the front end waiting for her. Since they were already out, Beth figured she might as well do as he said. They could have a little fun tonight and then it was back to business tomorrow.

"So what's there to do here?" she asked as she joined Tom. He took her hand in his, and they walked toward the Megaplex entrance. He had quickly acquired the habit of holding her hand when they walked, and it seemed she had acquired the habit of letting him. And liking it. His large hand held hers in a gentle grip, not too tight and not too loose. It was a grip that showed confidence but not dominance. It made her feel protected, yet respected.

And those feelings confused her.

So she pushed them out of her mind and focused on Tom's response to her question.

"Almost anything you want. Rock climbing, bumper boats, Go-Kart racing, miniature golf. They also have an arcade and a few midway-type rides, like the Ferris wheel and merry-go-round. What's your pleasure?"

Touching you all over. Wait, where did that come from? Didn't she just tell herself that tonight was about relaxing and having fun? She really had to pull herself together.

"I'm not big on heights, and I'm a little tired of motorized equipment after the traveling we did. I guess that leaves golf or the arcade. Which do you want?"

They had reached the ticket booth and joined the line to buy their passes. Tom still held her hand, but he turned to answer her.

"How about golf? I'd imagine it's much quieter on the greens than in the arcade. We can at least talk to each other there without shouting."

Beth agreed, and Tom purchased two tickets for the miniature golf course. They strolled, once again with joined hands, to the little shack near the first hole to pick up their clubs, balls, and scorecard. As they proceeded toward the first green, Beth decided to be honest with Tom.

"There's something I really need to tell you. Something that could affect the rest of the evening."

Tom stopped in his tracks and drew her to the side of the concrete path. "What is it? Are you feeling sick or something?"

He raised his hand to Beth's forehead, then smoothed her hair away from her face. His eyes showed concern.

Besides a few sore muscles, she felt physically okay. She was a little embarrassed, though. This was one of the reasons why she steered clear of personal involvements.

"I'm fine." She sighed. "But I think you should know that I've never played miniature golf before." There. It was out in the open.

"Ever?"

"Ever. In my whole life."

"Everybody's played mini golf. It's like the new place to go for teens, like drive-in movies used to be. How could you never have played before?"

Beth chose to share a bit of information, just so they could get on with the game. "My parents divorced when I was two, and I went to live with my mom in San Francisco. I never saw Dad much because he was gone on the road all the time. But when I was eight, I went to live with him."

"What happened when you were eight?"

"My mom was killed in a car accident. She was on her way home from work and a drunk driver hit her head-on. She was killed instantly."

"Oh, honey, I'm so sorry." Tom moved to hug her, but Beth held up her hands to ward him off.

"It's okay. I'm not telling you this to get sympathy. It was a long time ago. I'm telling you this so you'll know my childhood wasn't anything like yours or other normal people's. Between the ages of eight and eighteen I lived in more tour buses and hotel rooms than I can remember. I was educated by a long line of tutors, and I took standardized tests at whatever school was nearest to the concert hall. There was never a steady peer group for me to go to the movies, mall, or miniature golf with. I grew up with a revolving door of singers, groupies, and roadies around me. I'm sure a lot of people would kill to have a lifestyle like that, surrounded by fame and fortune, but I hated it. And I had no choice about living that way."

Beth stopped, aware she'd said way too much. Tom's expression was indecipherable, but he was probably thinking: *If you hated being on the road before, why did you become a roadie?* It was a legitimate question, but definitely not one she was willing to answer.

"So, can you show me how to play this game or what? Otherwise you won't have much competition and it'll be a boring waste of time for both of us."

•

Tom watched as Beth lifted her chin and glared at him, daring him to say something. He hated that she had to feel so defensive around him. He didn't want her to be ashamed of anything in her past. It was too bad certain parts of her upbringing upset her so much, but he sure was happy that she'd decided to spill information about herself of her own volition.

He'd reward her efforts by keeping his thoughts to himself and showing her how to have fun.

"Of course I'll show you. There's not much to it and you're a quick study. It's never too late to try new things, right?"

Tom escorted her to an area designated as the practice putting green. He demonstrated how to stand and swing the small club correctly. After observing him putt for a few minutes, Beth tried on her own. She used too much force in her swing at first but soon became adept in judging the amount of strength needed for various stroke distances.

After ten minutes of practice, Tom deemed her ready to begin. They proceeded to the first hole, which was a par three. Tom sunk his shot in three strokes, and Beth made it in four. He congratulated her on her good start, but she didn't seem happy about it.

As they moved from one green to another, it became evident that Beth was becoming increasingly agitated. And as her frustration level rose, her game got worse. By the time they'd completed the ninth hole, Beth was eight strokes behind Tom.

"Argh! Why can't I do this? I can balance million-dollar budgets with my eyes closed but I can't put a little ball into a freaking hole in the ground!" Beth looked about ready to toss her golf club into the air and stomp away, never to play the game again.

Tom glanced back to the eighth hole and saw there was nobody right behind them. "Look, we can spend a little time practicing again. You've got your long shots down fine but your short game is giving you problems." He dropped Beth's ball about four feet from the hole and laid his own club and ball off the edge of the green. Then he put his hands on her shoulders and guided her into position next to the ball so she could take a shot.

"You need to relax more. It looks to me like you're gripping the club too tightly and it's causing you to jerk it. The ball's not rolling smoothly into the hole—it's going right past it." Tom moved close behind Beth and skimmed his hands down her smooth arms. He wrapped his fingers around hers on the handle of the golf club.

"Now, just loosen up a bit. Your whole body is tense." Tom slid his arms from side to side, doing a couple of practice swings and forcing her to move in sync with him. He really should be taking his own advice. His body was getting stiffer with every swing of the club. Her soft bottom was cradled tightly against his groin, and every brush of her body against him made the fit of his pants become more and more snug.

He bent his head into the curve of her shoulder, inhaling the sweet raspberry fragrance of her shampoo. Oh, yeah, how he loved berries. Pushing her long blonde hair aside, he nuzzled the side of her neck, lost in the essence of her. "You smell absolutely terrific," he murmured softly next to her ear.

She quickly pulled from his embrace and moved out of reach. Her soft blue eyes were opened wide and there was a slight flush on her cheeks. She held the golf club out in a defensive stance. "Wh-what do you think you're doing, Tom?"

He decided to be blunt. "I think I was touching you and you were enjoying it. I'm sure you could tell that I was enjoying it a lot, too."

Her gaze slipped down to his crotch, his arousal still very much evident. The color in her cheeks darkened even more as her focus returned to his face. She slowly lowered the club back to the ground. "It doesn't matter if we both enjoyed ourselves for a moment. Nothing will come of it. I told you before, I'm not willing to get involved with anyone right now."

He really would have to find a way to convince her otherwise. But he didn't want to argue right now, so he backed off. "All right. Have it your way." Tom looked over his shoulder as a group of boisterous teenagers approached the fairway.

He turned back to Beth and said, "We need to move on to the next hole. Unless you want to give up for the night?"

She shook her head. "Hell, no. I'm not giving up. I will conquer this game if it kills me!" She moved toward the next complicated setup of hills, tunnels, and laughing clowns. "No clown will ever get the best of me again."

Tom wondered if that last statement applied to more than amusement park figurines, but the thought quickly faded as he watched Bethany lean down to place her ball into position on the green. Her short sundress pulled tight across her buttocks, outlining their firm shape and making his fingers itch to caress them. The hem rose just enough to make him wonder what she had on underneath her dress, because he couldn't detect any panty lines.

Beth straightened and tossed her hair back over her shoulder. She shifted her weight from one foot to another, eyeing the route from tee to hole. She took her first shot and landed the ball only two feet away from the cup. Soon after, Tom's ball came to rest at least six feet away from the target.

He'd obviously lost his concentration in the last few minutes.

"All right, you stupid ball. Go into the hole, will you?" Beth did a half-hearted Happy Gilmore impression by talking to the golf ball. But it seemed to work, because she easily sunk her putt. She raised her arm and pulled it down sharply, saying "Yes!" with a huge smile on her face.

The tenth hole was the start of some real competition. The incident on the ninth hole seemed to invigorate Beth and make her more focused while Tom couldn't make a decent shot to save his life. By the time they arrived at the eighteenth hole, Beth had caught up to Tom and the scores were dead even.

"Okay, buddy. This is it. Loser has to buy the ice cream cones, okay?" Beth was awfully sure of herself all of the sudden. Her confidence really turned him on, too. He just had to kiss her before the night was over. He had to.

Tom stepped up to place his ball on the green. The hole was a par two, and it looked simple enough. At this point it was a matter of principle. He had to win the game to show her that he could remain undistracted by her. If she could pretend then so could he.

He lined the shot up perfectly but at the last minute the ball curved. It came to rest a mere four inches from the cup. In order to clear the green, he quickly sank the putt, returning the ball to a collection tank. Tom turned to Beth and said, "Okay, darlin', see if you can top that." Then he walked to the side of the fairway to give her room to work.

Beth blew out a deep breath and rolled first her neck and then her bare shoulders back and forth. It was as if she were preparing for the Olympics of miniature golf she was so serious. But Tom was content to watch her graceful movements. It didn't matter how long it took her to make her shot.

Finally she was ready. She aligned her ball just so with the hole. She looked back and forth between the cup and the ball a few times. And then she swung.

Hole in one.

He couldn't believe it. She'd beat him by hitting a hole in one.

Beth shouted and screamed and jumped up and down, apparently not caring if other players thought she was nuts. "Oh, my God! Did you see that? I got a hole in one! That was so awesome!" She was magnificent in her excitement, and she continued her ravings as she happily pranced toward Tom.

"Thank you, thank you, thank you! That was so much fun! Thanks for bringing me here. It was great!" She threw her arms around Tom, enveloping him in a big hug.

Caught off guard by her exuberance, Tom quickly wrapped his arms around Beth, holding her close as she squeezed him tightly. She tilted her head back, saying teasingly, "I beat you fair and square. Now you owe me an ice cream."

Tom looked into her twinkling blue eyes, and then his gaze slid down to her smiling lips. Such luscious lips. He'd been thinking about this ever since they were interrupted in Jacksonville. He wasn't going to miss the opportunity again.

He moved one hand up to cradle the nape of her neck. He looked into her eyes one last time so that she'd clearly know his intentions. When Tom didn't see any obvious discomfort in her gaze, he finally did what he'd been dying to do since he'd laid eyes on Beth.

He kissed her.

Chapter Four

Beth closed her eyes and let herself enjoy Tom's mouth moving over hers. Why fight it anymore? She had as much right to feel wanted as anybody else did. And Tom obviously wanted her. His lips tenderly sipped at hers while his hands caressed her neck and back. Like she'd thought before, he had lots of talent in those body parts.

She tightened her arms around his neck, sinking her fingers into his short, thick hair. His tongue pressed against the seam of her lips and she gladly opened to allow him entrance. He tasted of man with a hint of steak sauce thrown in. And, oh boy, he could really make her forget her problems.

"Ooooo, baby." "That's right, get it on." "Can I get some of that when you're done with him, toots?" Loud whistles, grunts, and smooching noises accompanied the vulgar comments being shouted at Beth and Tom.

They jumped apart, staring at each other and breathing heavily. Beth tore her gaze from Tom's and glanced toward the group of teenage boys who had interrupted their kiss. The teenagers were still looking at the two of them, perhaps wondering if the intimate show they'd seen was going to be continued.

Tom, too, looked at the boys but then easily dismissed them. "C'mon, Bethany. Let's head out. I owe you an ice cream cone anyway."

They turned in their golf clubs and walked to the snack bar, holding hands all the while. It was amazing how fast she was getting used to this, how comfortable she was becoming with his touch. It was like they'd known each other far longer than a few days.

"You said you liked chocolate, right?"

Beth nodded absently in answer to Tom's question, still lost in her thoughts. She waited until he handed her a cone top-heavy with ice cream, then moved toward a nearby picnic table. He followed behind her with an equally large strawberry cone of his own.

They sat eating their frozen treats in silence for a while. Then Tom spoke.

"I don't regret what happened. I hope you don't either. And I'm still sticking to what I said before—we can take one day at a time. I don't expect to jump into a serious relationship right away. You said you didn't want that."

Beth listened as Tom spoke, slowly licking her ice cream and absorbing his words.

"But I haven't felt this attracted to a woman in a long time, and I'm hoping you'll give me—us—a chance to see where things can go. We can spend time together during the tour, and afterward who knows. Do you think we can do that? No pressure?" His hopeful expression didn't detract from his masculinity in the slightest.

Beth continued to lick her ice cream, noticing how Tom's eyes narrowed and focused on her tongue's movements. She gave an extra long stroke from the rim of the cone to the top of the dessert, just to see his reaction.

He lifted his darkened gaze to hers, accusing, "You're doing that on purpose. You want to drive me crazy."

Beth smiled. "Maybe. But it's no more than you're doing to me. And in answer to your question, yes. I'd like to spend more time with you." She figured it wouldn't hurt to have some fun over the next few weeks. She already knew nothing permanent could come of a relationship with Tom, but who said a short-term affair was out of the question? Maybe some commitment-free sex would help relieve her stress.

Tom smiled back at her, and they finished their desserts in comfortable silence. They leisurely strolled back to the truck, once again holding hands. Tom unlocked the vehicle and helped Beth inside, closing the door after her. But when he got behind the wheel, he didn't start the engine. Instead he just sat there, staring through the windshield, hands gripping the wheel so tightly that his knuckles were white. He sat there so long, so still, it made Beth nervous.

"Tom, what's wrong? Are you all right? Can I do anything to help?" Beth had no clue what was going on in his mind, and she was worried. She laid a hand on his arm, gently shaking it to gain his attention.

•

Tom jumped at Bethany's touch. He didn't realize he'd put himself so deep into a trance that he'd blocked out her presence. Of course, her presence was why he'd needed to meditate in the first place.

He put a hand over Beth's where it rested on his bare forearm. He could feel her touch all the way down to his toes. Instead of patting her hand, reassuring her that he was all right, he began caressing it. Running his fingers over her smooth skin and finally entwining their fingers together. He lifted her hand to his mouth and gave it a soft kiss.

"I'm okay, Beth. I just blocked out way too much that time."

She narrowed her eyes, still looking unsure. "'That time?' What do you mean? This happens to you a lot?" Her grip tightened around his hand, out of worry or fear he wasn't sure.

"Don't worry, it's nothing serious. It's not a medical condition or anything. It's just something I picked up in yoga class," he explained.

"You take yoga classes? And you drink milk with dinner, too. Are you a fitness nut or something?" Bethany looked a little uncomfortable at the thought.

"God, no," he said. "The yoga is something I did back in college. A girl I liked was into that stuff, and I kind of joined in order to impress her. Stupid, huh?"

She gave an exaggerated nod. "Oh, yeah. Pretty lame. I wouldn't have expected you to do something like that. She must have been really special."

Tom thought he detected a bit of jealousy in Beth's tone, and it encouraged him. He lifted her hand for another quick kiss, then said, "Actually, she wasn't all that great. We ended up going on a couple of dates but that was it. The chemistry just wasn't there between us. After the first couple weeks of yoga we weren't together anymore, but I found I really liked the sessions. Even though I never took another yoga class after that, I still use a few of the techniques I learned then."

"And that's what you were doing before? A yoga exercise?"

Tom nodded. "Yeah. I guess you can call it quasi-meditating.

I've sort of trained myself to block out the environment when I need to really focus on something. In college I used it to study during our neighbors' loud parties, and I've been able to use it when I'm writing lyrics and music, too. It helps me to stay in control of myself, stay on task."

Beth wore a look of bewilderment. "So why do it now? What was distracting you so much that you felt you had to zone out to la-la land?"

She honestly had no clue how alluring she was, how hard he was trying to stick to his word. No pressure, no rushing their relationship. That's what he'd told her, and that's what he intended to do. But she was waiting for an answer, and he figured he might as well lay it on the line.

"You were distracting me. I had to meditate in order to keep my hands off you."

•

Beth's jaw dropped open in astonishment, and her hand went lax within Tom's grip. He couldn't be serious. "What the hell are you talking about? Didn't we just agree to spend time together, get to know each other?"

"Yeah, but we agreed to take it slow. I have no right to pressure you, and I didn't want to push you into a lot of physical stuff right off the bat."

Beth couldn't believe the integrity of the man. Or it could be stupidity. She wasn't quite sure yet. "Well, I certainly didn't plan to have sex with you tonight, for Christ's sake, but a few more kisses wouldn't frighten me. Going slow does not require that you put yourself into a catatonic state!"

Tom looked at her with a doubtful expression. "So I can kiss you again? You won't be offended? Or feel pressured?"

She actually wished at that moment that Tom wasn't such a nice guy. She was going to bash his head in if he didn't stop pussyfooting around.

"You'd better kiss me. And after all this discussion about it, it better be good!"

Tom grinned and stretched over the center console of the truck. "I'll do my best."

He cupped her chin in his wide hand, his grin fading away as he stared into her eyes. Beth waited with anticipation. Finally he dropped his liquid chocolate gaze to her lips and slowly lowered his mouth to hers.

It was even better than it'd been before. Beth closed her eyes in ecstasy as Tom's lips gently moved over hers. She enjoyed his easy pace for a few moments but soon wanted more. She eagerly opened to him, thrusting her tongue into his mouth, wanting to explore every bit of him.

He was absolutely the best kisser she'd ever encountered in her life. Not that she'd kissed all that many guys, but the few she'd let go that far had nothing on Tom. He was amazing, bringing her blood to a raging boil with every swipe of his tongue inside her mouth, every nip of his perfect teeth on her swollen lips.

Tom pulled back, breathing heavily. "Are you okay?"

Beth nodded shakily, panting. "I'm great."

She pulled his head back down to hers, digging her fingers into his hair. She placed soft kisses over his stubbly chin and cheeks, caressing his scalp all the while. Then she zeroed in on his gorgeous mouth again, desperate for the feel of his kiss.

Tom groaned deep in his chest and roughly pulled her over the center console and onto his lap. He fumbled under the seat for levers, finally succeeding in sliding his seat all the way back and into a reclining position. Beth readjusted her long legs, folding them up behind her so that she straddled Tom's hips on the narrow seat. It wasn't exactly a comfortable position, but she was willing to endure it if it meant continuing to kiss him.

She leaned over him, smoothing her fingers over the masculine contours of his chest. Firm yet not overly muscular. Perfect. But she needed to feel him without the interference of a cloth barrier. Grabbing the hem of his polo shirt, Beth tugged it up under his armpits. She could see a light dusting of dark hair in the center of his chest, extending outward to sprinkle around his small male nipples. Using the dim lights of the parking lot to guide her, she leaned down to suck on one. It sprang to erectness beneath her tongue.

Tom let out another groan, entwining his long fingers into her hair, pressing her tighter against his chest. She caressed his other nipple, using her fingertips to draw circles around it and gently tug on its tip. Apparently she'd found a very sensitive area. She switched the positions of her hand and mouth, wanting to give each nub equal attention.

After a few moments Tom pulled her head away, making her groan this time. He gave her a quick kiss and then sat her up straight, away from him. "Turnabout is fair play."

He tugged the straps of her sundress off her shoulders. Beth knew a brief moment of insecurity but it passed as soon as Tom pushed down the fitted bodice of her dress. The parking lot was practically empty and the truck had tinted windows. No one could see them even if they walked right next to the vehicle.

"Beautiful." He filled his hands with her breasts, cupping them with tenderness. He grazed her nipples with his thumbs, quickly making them taut. Beth shivered in reaction, having never felt this turned on so easily. Not even with Eric, when she'd thought she loved him.

Beth immediately slammed the door shut on any thought of that man. He was no longer in her life, thank God. Tom was here now, and he deserved every bit of her concentration.

"Come here," he murmured hoarsely. "I want to taste you."

He wrapped his arms around her back, gently drawing her down. He took a hardened nipple into his hot mouth, making her cry out in shock. It felt so damn good. He licked her breasts over and over again with his rough tongue, alternating with gentle nips and tugs of his fingers—just as she had done to him. Obviously he enjoyed doing it as much as she had.

Her long blonde hair flowed around his head, tangling in her fingers as they delved into his thick, dark locks. She had to hold onto him somehow because she felt like she was going to fly off into the night sky. She needed to keep herself grounded.

Perhaps the large erection pressing against her inner thighs could serve as a lightning rod.

Tom lifted his face from her breasts, setting her back so he could look into her eyes. "We have to stop."

Beth uttered a sound of disgust. "Why? What's the problem now?"

She was seriously getting irritated at the games he was playing. Did he want her or not? His body was saying yes but his mouth kept contradicting that message.

"We don't have any condoms and we're in the middle of a public parking lot. Not to mention the fact that you just told me ten minutes ago that you weren't going to have sex with me tonight. I'm not willing to rush you into something you'd regret in the morning, no matter how much you think you want it right now."

Tom waited for Beth's reaction. She sat, looking down at his handsome face, feeling how turned on he still was. How turned on they both still were.

But he was right. They weren't prepared for practicing safe sex, and making love with Tom for the first time in the middle of the Megaplex of Fun's parking lot really wasn't appropriate. But that didn't mean she wouldn't have tried harder to seduce him if they'd been in a more secluded area. Once she'd given herself permission to pursue a relationship with Tom, albeit a short-term one, she was willing to go for it wholeheartedly.

Beth leaned down to give Tom one last, lingering kiss before moving back to the passenger seat. Shaking the kinks out of her cramped legs, she admitted, "You're right. This isn't the time or the place. We got a little carried away."

She glanced over to Tom, only to see his gaze fixed upon her quivering breasts. She hadn't straightened her sundress and the motions of her shifting legs made her upper body move, too. She froze in place, her desire swiftly rising again.

But Tom shook himself out of his lust-induced fog and readjusted his seat to the proper positions for driving. Then he reached across the console to pull her dress into place. He tugged his own shirt down and let out a deep breath, resting his forearms against the steering wheel.

"I guess we can agree we've got some awesome chemistry." He turned to her and continued, "We've just gotta find the right conditions for letting the fireworks happen."

He reached over and tugged on her hand, bringing it to his mouth for an affectionate smack. "But that won't be tonight, darlin', so we should probably get back to the auditorium. It's pretty late now and tomorrow will be another long day."

He placed her palm on his firm thigh then released her hand to start the truck. While her pulse slowly returned to normal, Beth continued to watch Tom's face as he maneuvered out of the parking lot and onto the main road. He was so confident in everything he did. Driving, playing golf, performing on stage, making love. When she'd asked him earlier if he was a fitness nut, she'd been very afraid his answer would be yes. That would have taken him one step closer to perfection. And someone as messed up as she was couldn't be involved with someone who was near perfect.

•

He was a basket case. He couldn't believe he'd lost control of the situation so quickly. He honestly hadn't meant for things to go that far.

Tom surreptitiously glanced at Bethany out of the corner of his eye, not wanting her to get self-conscious. But he couldn't stop looking at her. She was so beautiful. And passionate. He could still taste the intensity of her kisses.

Right now she was looking out the side window, probably trying to pull herself together. Just like he was.

Her hand remained on his thigh, burning him with its heat. Periodically it would clench at his flesh through his khakis. He wondered what thoughts still remained in her mind to make that happen.

Trying to stay focused on the road in front of him, Tom reflected upon how different Beth was from other women he'd known. His last long-term relationship had ended almost a year ago, when Marissa claimed she'd had it with him. She wasn't going to waste her life, sitting by while he played at being a bigshot country singer.

Marissa hadn't understood that performing was Tom's dream— one he intended to make come true on a larger scale. He didn't sing in clubs on the weekends because it was a frivolous hobby or an easy way to get laid. It made him happy. It made him feel like he was on top of the world, watching as people enjoyed the music he composed and played.

He had met Marissa in Savannah when she'd caught Roadhouse's performance one evening. A mutual friend had introduced them, and they hit it off right away. At first she'd loved the idea that her boyfriend was in a band, probably because she was able to get into clubs at no charge and usually enjoyed free drinks, too. But gradually, over the year and a half they were together, the novelty had worn off. Marissa had grown weary of watching Tom perform every weekend in local, and sometimes not so local, clubs.

She nagged at Tom to take time off from performing so they could have a real vacation together, or at least a real date. And when that tactic didn't work, she tried to convince his father to increase his hours at the family store. She figured if he worked a lot in the hardware store during the week he'd need time off on the weekend to recuperate. Preferably with her.

That didn't work either.

Tom's father had refused her request. And his father had told Tom of Marissa's attempt to interfere with his work schedule. That revelation had led to their first big argument, and the relationship hadn't lasted long afterward.

Marissa had tried to smother Tom's feelings of happiness and fulfillment. She tried to take away his freedom to pursue his dream in life. And he refused to give up his dream for any woman.

Tom glanced at Bethany one more time as they neared the Macon City Auditorium. Now she was looking straight ahead through the windshield.

"Hey, are you okay? You've been awfully quiet."

She turned and gave him a small smile. "Yeah, I'm fine. I guess all the excitement and adrenaline from today suddenly wore off. I feel like I've been hit by a ton of bricks."

"Don't worry. We're almost back to our home away from home."

Tom parked the SUV in its assigned spot and turned off the engine. He left the vehicle and walked around to meet Beth as she stepped out. Then he escorted her back to the RV she shared with Liz and Hannah. The only light visible inside was the small kitchenette bulb she'd left on over the sink. It cast a faint glow over Beth's features as Tom stopped outside the door.

"I had a really great time tonight," he said. He raised a hand to trail his fingertips over her soft cheek, loving the feel of her.

Beth's wide eyes stared up at him. "I did, too. I can't wait to see where things go from here."

Her tone wasn't the least bit teasing. It was just honest enthusiasm that he heard, tempting him to sample her lips one last time before he retired to his lonely bed.

"Things are only going to get better, sweetheart. No doubt about it."

Tom lowered his lips to Beth's. What was meant to be a gentle good night kiss quickly flared into a passionate engagement of lips, teeth, and tongues. Hands tangled in hair while mouths converged in an endless quest to sate their hunger for each other.

"Oh, sorry guys. We didn't mean to interrupt."

"Yeah, we'll just slip inside and pull the curtains. Then you can continue as you were."

Tom slowly lifted his head and unwrapped Beth's hair from his fingers. He looked over to where Liz and Hannah stood a few feet away.

"That's okay, ladies. We were just saying good night anyway." He stepped away from Beth but caught her hands as they slowly slid down his chest. She still looked a bit distracted from their kiss.

"Okay, Tom. If you say so. But I don't think anyone's ever told me good night in quite that way." Hannah wiggled her eyebrows at him and beamed a huge grin as she and Liz made their way past to enter the RV.

"That's probably because you didn't stop talking long enough to give him a chance!" The redhead stuck her tongue out at him in reply before closing the door, leaving Tom and Beth alone once again.

"I like them. They're really nice. And they sing beautifully, too."

Tom returned his gaze to Bethany, who was now looking extremely tired again. He leaned down to give her a quick peck, intentionally not letting his lips linger. He didn't want to risk having their kiss interrupted for the third time in one night.

"Yeah, they're both great. Roadhouse was lucky to find them. But that's enough talk. I think it's time you finally got to bed for the evening." Tom clarified his words. "To sleep, I mean."

Beth offered a weary smile. "I knew what you meant."

"Okay, then. I'll see you tomorrow. Sleep well."

Tom allowed one last brush of their lips before turning Beth toward the door. He watched as she pulled it open and stepped inside, glancing back to wish him a final farewell. "Good night, Tom."

The door closed and Tom was alone. Slowly he walked back to the band's motor home, softly whistling all the while.

Chapter Five

Beth stood near the stage of the Macon City Auditorium, watching as the members of Roadhouse proceeded through their pre-concert sound check. As she looked on, Tom strummed a few chords on a midnight blue electric guitar. Then he adjusted some knobs on the attached amplifier and tried the melody again.

His long fingers moving over the instrument's strings evoked memories of how those hands had felt running over her body last night. What a fantastic evening it had been. After she'd made her decision to pursue a brief relationship with Tom, it'd felt like a giant weight had been lifted off her shoulders. She finally had a distraction to keep her mind off the crazy jumble her life had become in the last few months.

And what a distraction he was.

Dressed in his usual casual stage attire of T-shirt and jeans, Tom looked scrumptious. And not only was he hot-looking, but he could make the sweetest music she had ever heard.

Having grown up traveling with a roadie-turned-road manager father, she loved listening to all types of music. What she'd told Tom when they first met, about not listening to country music, was a lie. She actually preferred the simple tunes about everyday life when she was in a sad mood and needed to be uplifted. Traditional country songs reminded her of the basic pleasures in life and how easy it was to forget about the small things which made you smile.

But Beth really wouldn't consider the music that Roadhouse played true country. Country rock was probably more appropriate, because while the songs they sang still revolved around the joys and sorrows of daily existence, the men performed with a definite edge. Roadhouse exuded so much energy when they were on stage that their concerts were the complete opposite of relaxing.

Even now, Tom was whaling out a solo on his guitar and looking for all the world like a wild rock star. He bent his trim body around and let out kicks like a hyperactive child who'd consumed too much sugar. She knew how great of shape that body was in because she'd felt it against her last night. And she couldn't wait to find out what kind of contortions they could engage in together.

"They sound good, don't they?"

Beth jumped at the question, having been so consumed with watching the activity on stage that she hadn't heard anyone come up beside her. She reluctantly pulled her gaze from Tom and turned to face her father.

"Yeah, they do. And they seem to love what they're doing."

"Well, of course they love it. Anybody in this business has to enjoy what they're doing to put up with all the crap they'll get, both from the public and the recording industry. They'd have to be insane otherwise."

She remained silent, and George offered another comment. "I hear you and Tom had a date last night."

Beth rolled her eyes and let out a resigned sigh. She'd known this would happen. Between Tom's asking Mike for a suggestion on where to take her to dinner and Liz and Hannah's teasing after she'd entered the RV last night, Beth was sure the news would get around to the rest of the crew.

"We had dinner together, yes."

"Dinner? I heard you got back kind of late. Did they have to kill the cow before they cooked it?" Her father raised an eyebrow and gave a teasing smile, obviously hoping for more information.

"And we played miniature golf afterward, okay? Anything else you want to know?" Not that she would tell him. Beth was only willing to share so much with George. The intimate details of her evening with Tom were her business only.

"Yeah. How serious is this? Am I finally going to walk my baby girl down the aisle?"

Beth shook her head and let out another sigh, this time of exasperation. "Dad, we've eaten a couple of meals together. He's a nice guy, and we like each other. That's it. Don't make more of this than it really is. You know I'm only here for a little while."

"Why do you say that? There's nothing holding you in San Francisco anymore. You could work anywhere in the country with your accounting degree. And you were great at your job. It was the circumstances that forced you to leave, not your poor job performance."

"Yes, Dad, indirectly it was my performance." And lack of judgment, she added silently. "Besides, I'm not even sure if I want to keep working as an accountant. The whole episode left a bad taste in my mouth."

Her father reached out and laid his hands on Beth's shoulders, giving her a little shake. "Now, Bethany, you worked damn hard to get where you are. Don't let one bad experience sour you on something you honestly enjoyed doing. Just use these next few weeks to take a break and relax your mind. Maybe another opportunity will jump out in front of you."

Beth gave George a quick hug and then stepped back. "You're right, Dad. This is my time to relax and do something totally different for a while. Have some fun before returning to the rat-race of corporate finance."

"Any of that fun going to be had with Tom?" Her father seemed hopeful for an affirmative answer.

"I'd like to say yes, but we'll see what happens." Beth shot a quick glance at Tom, now busy wrapping up the rehearsal on stage, before giving her father an earnest look. "And Tom doesn't know about what happened in San Francisco, so make sure you don't say anything in front of him, okay? Promise?"

Her father dodged her question by throwing out one of his own. "Why haven't you said anything to him? You didn't do anything wrong."

"I haven't said anything because it's not his business. I consider him a friend, but it's not something he needs to know. It's not like we're going to see each other once this tour is over, so why share unnecessary information?" The thought of not seeing Tom on a daily basis sent a twinge of pain through her heart, and Beth was shocked. She didn't think she'd grown that attached to the man after less than a week. Obviously she was wrong. "Anything that develops between us will be finished in a few weeks."

And Beth knew that, logically, that was the way it had to be.

"Maybe you should tell that to Tom." George tipped his head to the side, and Beth turned to see Tom approaching from the stage. There was a smile on his face as he sauntered their way, his eyes on her the whole time. "I don't think he has the same idea you do about your relationship."

•

Tom kept his gaze on Bethany as he neared, watching as a slight flush arose over her face. Good. He wanted her to feel as unsettled as he did, especially after what had happened between them the previous night.

"Hi," he said softly, staring into her wide blue eyes. Getting lost in them. Wanting to stay lost in them …

"A-hem."

The less than subtle disturbance made Tom tear his gaze from Beth's in order to give a nod to her father. "Hey, George." Then he turned back to Beth.

"Well, I can see I'm not needed here. I'll just go play with some equipment somewhere." And with an indulgent smile on his face George ambled off, leaving them alone.

"Oh. Bye, Dad!" Beth belatedly called out after him, casting only a quick look in her father's direction before returning her focus to Tom.

"You sounded good up there." A hesitant smile accompanied Bethany's words, but her gaze slid down, away from his. It was a sure sign she was nervous, and that was the one thing Tom didn't want her to be.

"Hey," he said, reaching out to take her hand. "Are you okay? No regrets about last night?" He slowly rubbed his thumb over her skin, waiting for an indication that things were still going well between them.

"Oh, no! Of course not!" She looked surprised he'd even asked the question. "But, um, I didn't think you'd come talk to me, and, you know, draw more attention to the two of us, together." Beth glanced over to the stage where his pals were avidly watching Tom's activities. Then she lowered her eyes again.

"Hey," Tom said again, this time in a not so gentle way. He used an insistent finger to urge her chin up, forcing Beth to meet his gaze. "What goes on between us stays between us. The guys can think what they like. Anything that happens between you and me is our business only. They're my friends and my band mates. They're not my conscience."

Beth frowned at his words, drawing her dark blonde brows

together and causing cute little wrinkles to appear on her forehead. He wanted to lick them away.

"Does that mean you're going against your conscience if you get involved with me? You think it's wrong?"

Tom let out a frustrated sigh. "Absolutely not. Bad choice of words. The only thing I meant was that I have relationships with whomever I choose. My friends have no influence over that part of my life. And besides, I told you before—we already are involved. I would've thought last night proved that to you."

He tugged Beth's hand up for a kiss and then pulled her along behind him, heading toward the backstage area. "Be back in a few!" he called to his band mates as he and Beth passed by.

"Where are we going?" Her question was meaningless since Beth showed no resistance to coming with him.

Tom pushed her into the first dressing room he came to. Thankfully it was empty.

"What are we doing in here?" Beth looked curious but not uncomfortable.

Tom followed her into the small area and closed the door behind him. "You seemed tense in front of everybody, so I figured we could find some private space for a few minutes. But mostly I just couldn't wait to do this..."

Tom hauled Beth into his arms and lowered his mouth to taste the sweet lips he'd been craving since last night. She quickly opened to him, allowing full access to the deep recesses of her mouth.

He wrapped his hand around her long blonde braid and tugged, slanting her head to obtain better contact. Bethany's arms wound around his neck, her fingers tousled his hair. She definitely was a full participant in this embrace. Glad to know her interest hadn't waned since yesterday.

Tom lifted his head to gulp a much-needed breath before returning his mouth to Beth's. He turned around to press her up against the door, then moved his hands down to the hem of her T-shirt.

"Okay?" he asked in a guttural voice.

She nodded jerkily, her breaths coming in harsh gasps.

He pushed his hands under her lime green shirt, sliding them over the warm, smooth skin of her belly, then up toward her firm, high breasts. His lips took a slow, meandering path over her face, touching on her well-defined cheekbones, her pert nose, the area of her brow that he'd wanted to lick earlier. There were no lines there now. Nope, she had no worries at all that he could discern.

His mouth closed over hers at the same time his fingers closed around her breasts. He remembered how they'd looked and tasted. He wanted to taste them again. He pushed Beth's shirt up, reached to release the front clasp of her satin ivory-colored bra.

"Hey, Tommy, you in there?"

A loud banging on the door at Beth's back accompanied Leo's intrusive question.

"You wanna grab something to eat before we go on? George ordered in some Chinese."

Tom lowered his hands to Beth's hips and rested his forehead against hers. He closed his eyes and let out a haggard breath.

Bad timing once again, but it really was for the best. Bethany deserved better than to be groped in a dressing room while various cohorts milled nearby. If she still intended to have sex with him, he was going to make sure it happened in a relatively classy place. Not backstage at the Macon City Auditorium.

"Yeah," he called back to his friend. "I'll be right there."

Tom adjusted Beth's shirt and stepped back from her. She looked just as dazed as he felt. When he kissed her he lost all touch with reality, and Leo's knock had brought him back with a crash.

"Sorry about that. I didn't mean to get so carried away. Not here, anyway."

Beth's gaze sharpened. "I'm glad you added that last part. If you'd tried to apologize yet again for kissing me, I would've clocked you. In case you didn't notice, I wasn't telling you to stop."

"I know. You were right there with me." Tom grinned. "I guess you really do find me irresistible."

Beth rolled her eyes and playfully slapped his arm. "Oh, pul-leeze," she said. "You just happened to be available at the moment. I could suck face with any one of a million guys if I really wanted to."

Tom's grin faltered a bit, but he quickly caught it. He knew Beth meant it as a joke, but he also realized the truth. She was so beautiful and funny and intelligent that she really could be with whomever she chose. He felt lucky she'd picked him.

"C'mon," he said, pulling Beth away from the door so he could open it. "Let's go get some grub before all the orange chicken and egg rolls are gone. I need more than rice to sustain me."

Beth followed him into the hall but then stopped.

"I need to go check out some lines. Cole thought he'd seen some fraying but he can't remember exactly where. I told him I'd help him look."

Tom was disappointed he wouldn't be seeing her again until after the performance, but he understood. Beth wasn't one to take her responsibilities lightly.

"All right. We definitely don't want any equipment malfunctions when we're on." He leaned down for a final kiss. "Go make us look good."

Beth walked away, moving back toward the auditorium. But he still heard her parting comment. "Hmmph. You do that just fine on your own."

A huge smile spread across Tom's face as he headed toward the makeshift mess area down the hall.

·

There were five good-looking guys on the stage six rows in front of her, but the girl's attention unwaveringly remained on only one of them. Tom Crowley. Her soul mate.

He was everything she could ever want. Handsome, gifted, and above all, sweet. She'd known he would be, but meeting him the other night in Jacksonville had definitely confirmed her beliefs.

His smile had made her all warm inside, and the way he'd signed her concert program solidified her notion that he was just as enamored with her. "Happy to meet you." It seemed like a simple generic greeting at first glance, but she understood the hidden meaning behind it.

She knew that Tom, nice guy that he was, wouldn't want to come on too strong with her at their first meeting. Even though he felt all the urges that she did, and he knew they were meant to be together, Tom wouldn't rush things. He would woo her slowly and steadily, showing his appreciation of her devotion by singing to her and buying her sweet little tokens of affection.

Knowing Tom was a struggling musician, she didn't expect, or want, extravagant gifts from him. She had no interest in his moneymaking potential. She had enough money to support both of them.

And that was one reason to be thankful to her parents. The only reason, actually. Harold and Edith Sommersby were definitely not your run-of-the-mill parents. Having inherited a fortune from his father, in addition to making millions more dollars through his own corporation, Harold was not a man to sit around letting life pass him by.

No, right now her parents were touring Europe and the Far East, probably for at least their third time. They had a globetrotting lifestyle that didn't bring them back home to Georgia all that often. They usually stayed long enough to attend a few important society gatherings, say hello to their only daughter, and deposit money into her bank account. They wouldn't be returning to the States for at least two months.

Which suited her just fine.

This way no one was around to interfere with her plans for the next month and a half. She was free to attend every single performance of Roadhouse's premiere tour. With each concert and encounter with Tom, she knew their relationship would become deeper and stronger.

And by the end of Roadhouse's tour, Tom Crowley would love her as much as she loved him.

Chapter Six

Beth was too inexperienced to realize the initial string of concerts had gone too well. Or maybe she'd been having such fun with Tom that she'd mistakenly donned rose-colored glasses toward the whole tour. Regardless, a series of mishaps over the last three performances changed her outlook pretty quick.

At least Beth felt secure in knowing nothing had gone wrong because of her. It was just bad luck showing its face at inopportune times.

First, the tractor-trailer hauling Roadhouse's equipment to Columbia got a flat tire. Well, actually, it was four flat tires. Some jokester had thought it was funny to throw a bucket of three-inch nails across a dark highway to see what would happen.

The simultaneous leakage of so many tires at once could've resulted in tragedy, and only Sal's many years of driving big rigs saved both his life and the precious cargo he carried.

As it was, a delay of several hours occurred while police reports were filled out and a service truck arrived to change the tires. Beth and the rest of the crew had to work their asses off to ensure Roadhouse's performance proceeded on schedule, but they did it.

Then, in Charlotte, an unexpected late spring storm brought thunder, lightning, and torrential rains. The house lights flickered twice while the crew set up, causing concern of a power outage. Everyone also wondered if the awful weather would deter fans from traveling to the show.

They needn't have worried about anything.

Just as eerily as it had blown in, the storm disappeared about an hour before show time. And the theater was packed with enthusiastic fans who demanded not one but two encores.

The last bit of misfortune involved the entire band. All five

Roadhouse musicians came down with food poisoning after consuming a catered meal from a local Italian restaurant.

Luckily the crew members had all decided on deli sandwiches that day. Also fortunate was that Marty had scheduled their day off in Richmond, giving the band time to recover before performing at the Carpenter Center.

Today, Tom sat next to Beth near the rear of the remodeled Hippodrome Theatre in Baltimore.

She'd been working on the final connections of wires to the mixing board. Tom had arrived early to sound check, and he'd sought her out as soon as he'd entered the theatre, stopping only to grab a cold drink for each of them.

Aside from the time he'd been ill, Tom had spent most of his waking hours with her. Beth realized as the days passed how much she really liked him. He impressed her with his sense of humor and amazing talent. He thrilled her with every touch, which, unfortunately, hadn't been as numerous as she would've liked.

At the moment he was holding her hand, talking about his childhood hobby of fishing and how much he'd like to get back to it again once his music career got established. While one part of her loved his familiar contact and the easy way he shared personal information with her, another part of Beth was troubled.

Tom's childhood and dreams were the extreme opposite of hers. He'd had a stable upbringing, and she'd been shuffled from one town to another, one performance to another. Now, when she was looking for a safe, solitary existence, he was embarking on the unsteady journey of every hopeful musician who longed to hit the big time. And, of course, he'd have to do whatever it took to remain there.

It was guaranteed their affair would be a short one. If it ever got off the ground, that is. The tour's run of bad luck over the past week seemed to extend itself to Tom and Beth's relationship as well.

Not a single opportunity had arisen where they could do more than kiss. Now that their interest in each other was common knowledge, the band and crew members appeared to be sabotaging Tom and Beth's attempts to be alone.

She wasn't sure whether it was deliberate or not, but the end result was the same: No sex yet.

And she was getting more frustrated with each passing day.

"I'd love to take you fishing in the Adirondacks. Our drummer, Dylan, grew up in New York, and he knows the best places to go. I think you'd like it."

Beth was jerked back to the present at Tom's comment. "Excuse me?"

"I said, I want to take you fishing in upstate New York. Dylan could tell us where to go."

That's what she'd thought he said. What the heck was he thinking?

"Uh, Tom. I've never been fishing in my life. Unless you count those mechanical carnival games with the floating plastic fish. But that was almost twenty years ago, and I sucked at it anyway."

She was babbling, but Beth didn't know what else to say. Hadn't she made it clear to Tom that there was no future for them after the tour?

Apparently she hadn't been clear enough.

But, since she didn't want to upset the general amity of the moment, Beth decided not to push the issue. She would just play along with him.

"Like I told you, I haven't gone for a long time, either," Tom was saying. "I think it's like riding a bike—you never forget once you master it. And I was damn good, if I do say so myself. I'd enjoy showing you all the tricks I know."

Beth knew he was referring to fishing, but she chose to believe he knew quite a few sexual tricks as well. God willing, she would learn some of those very soon.

"What did you do for fun growing up?"

Huh? The man jumped from one topic to another like a slingshot.

"What?"

"You didn't fish. You didn't play miniature golf. So what did you do for recreation?"

Tom waited patiently for her reply while Beth tried to wipe the astonished look off her face.

Didn't he realize that her entire adolescence had been a recreational experience? And not by her choice.

She'd had to work very hard to remain focused on schoolwork, but Beth had been determined to get in to a respectable college. She'd been accepted to Stanford, so at least part of her life had gone to plan.

"Um, I was on the road with my dad, remember?" Beth fumbled for a nice way to remind Tom that her childhood hadn't been remotely like his. "We didn't exactly have a lot of leisure time." And it still hurt to think about all she'd missed out on growing up.

"Hey, we're on tour now. And if you have time to be with me, then I'm sure when you were young, George had time to spend with you." Tom's chiding tone didn't sit well with Beth. What did he know? He hadn't been there.

Memories of her teenage years crowded her: Trying to study on the bus as spontaneous jam sessions broke out. Being watched by a hotel maid-turned-babysitter while after-concert parties transpired down the hall or on another floor. Crying herself to sleep because she had no friends or mother to confide in.

She'd only survived her first menstrual period because the bassist of a long-defunct all-girl rock band had helped her through it.

It had been nothing but hell growing up on the road, and she never wanted to live that way again.

"My father dedicated his time to his job. There wasn't anything left for me." The words tumbled out of their own accord, but Beth quickly tried to bluff her way out of it. Tried to mask how deeply the truth of her upbringing had hurt her.

She flashed Tom a weak smile. "Good thing he could call in favors to get me a job, huh? All that dedication paid off in the end."

Tom's probing stare said she hadn't fooled him in the slightest. But he decided to let it rest for now, moving on to yet another topic. "Do you need another soda?"

He stood up, drawing her gaze once again to his sexy body, adorned as usual in jeans and T-shirt. This one was a dark blue color which matched the shade of his electric guitar.

Oh, yeah, she couldn't wait to get some of that. Soon, please.

Beth shook her head. "No, thanks. Break's almost over anyway. We need to get finished so you guys can awe your next crowd of fans."

Tom's eyes scanned the activities in the theatre before returning to Beth. "I'll grab you another in case you change your mind later. It doesn't feel like the AC is working right in here, and the afternoon's only gonna get hotter. June in the south is a nightmare."

With that, Tom strode away toward the refreshment table that had been set up for the crew and band members. The iced drinks had come in handy during the last few concerts. He was right about that, at least: Summer in the south sucked. After living in San Francisco seven years, Beth was used to cool weather, fog, and drizzle. She didn't know if she would ever adjust to the heat and humidity of the southeast.

But what was she thinking? In three weeks she'd be back on the West Coast. Searching for a job ... searching for a life.

Okay, maybe that wasn't such a cheerful thought. Better to think about the present. Her roadie responsibilities. Tom. Sex.

Sex with Tom.

Beth didn't think she'd ever wanted physical intimacy with a man as much as she did right now. What was so attractive about him anyway?

Yeah, he was gorgeous. And funny. And sexy.

But he also drove her nuts with his presumptions about her life. She thought they'd gotten past that the first day they'd met, but his chastising words about her childhood proved her wrong.

Maybe he loved the musician life so much that he didn't want to hear her badmouth any part of it. If she had any real dreams at the moment, she wouldn't want anyone to bash them into the ground, either.

So okay, she wouldn't say anything else about her dysfunctional upbringing, and Tom could idealize the lifestyle as much as he wanted. It was fine with her.

It wasn't as if she'd be around him forever.

And maybe, if pressed, she would be able to remember a few good times on the road with her father. Maybe.

But she doubted it.

A weary sigh escaped Beth, and she rubbed her aching neck. At least while she was on the road this time she was doing something productive. But after years of academics and office work she wasn't used to manual labor, even the comparatively small amount she was directed to do.

She felt better knowing the rough times of the tour seemed to be past. They'd had no equipment, vehicle, health, or weather problems since arriving in Baltimore this morning. Tonight's performance looked to be another success. And maybe, just maybe, she could convince Tom to sneak away with her after the show. To someplace private.

Beth closed her eyes, her body shivering with anticipation of what hopefully would occur that night.

But then a muted conversation to her far right cut through the pleasant images running through her head.

Beth looked over to see Tom talking to two guys in dark suits. She'd never seen the men before, and curiosity kept her watching the trio.

Tom gestured to Beth with one hand, easily holding two full soda bottles in the other. The men observed his directive and then started toward her with Tom just a step behind.

What now?

Beth should've known things couldn't get better so quickly.

But she hadn't imagined they'd get horribly worse.

•

Tom felt no qualms in following the two men back to Beth. Although they hadn't introduced themselves, he knew they must be here in an official capacity. They couldn't have entered the theatre without showing identification at the entrance.

What did they want with her?

If Bethany didn't want him to know, she could tell him to leave. But until that happened, he was staying close.

Beth stood and stepped into the aisle as they approached. She looked to him and raised an eyebrow. Tom shrugged his shoulders and shook his head in response. He had no idea what they wanted either.

"Ms. Miller?" The older of the two men held out his hand to Beth. "I'm Detective Halsey with the Baltimore PD."

His head glinted in the light where it wasn't covered with thinning gray hair. Halsey looked like he could've retired years ago but had enjoyed the doughnut shops too much to leave.

Beth hesitantly shook the man's hand, flashing yet another inquisitive look toward Tom, who was just as clueless as she was.

Halsey nodded toward his companion. "This is Detective Chen."

In contrast to his partner, the trim Asian-American officer looked fresh out of the academy. He smiled and offered his hand.

"Ms. Miller."

Evidently neither detective felt the need to greet Tom, so he simply deposited the drinks he carried into a vacant seat, moved to Beth's side, and waited for them to explain their presence.

"Do you guys have identification?" Beth's tone indicated she didn't trust the men. But she got the results she wanted since they pulled out their badges for her to study. "What do you want?"

Tom hadn't seen such a poor attitude from Beth since their first meeting, and the unfamiliar agitation he saw in her triggered his own. Just what the hell was going on here?

"Ms. Miller, we need to speak with you." Detective Halsey shot a look at Tom. "Alone."

Bethany seemed to steel herself. Against what, he wasn't sure. "Whatever you need to say to me can be said in front of Tom. Now, what is it you need to tell me?"

Tom slowly let out the breath he didn't know he'd been holding. Maybe now he'd find out what was behind Beth's hesitancy about their relationship. Sure, she still wanted to get physical, but nothing more.

And, for some reason, that bothered the crap out of him.

Any other guy would jump at the chance to have a purely sexual relationship with a gorgeous, unattached female. But no, not him.

Ever since he'd met her, Tom had wanted to know all he could about this guarded woman. And he was about to discover another piece of the puzzle that was Bethany Miller.

The younger detective spoke up. "It's about Eric Sharpe."

Beth's face paled at the name, and Tom quickly put his arms around her, thinking she might faint.

Who was Eric Sharpe? And why did Beth have such an intense reaction to the mention of his name?

An unfamiliar wave of jealousy swept over Tom, accompanied by a touch of hurt when Beth pulled out of his hold.

She cleared her throat with a rough cough. "Um." Another cough. "What—what does that have to do with me anymore? I was cleared of all charges."

What?

Tom's jaw dropped, and he snapped his head to stare at Beth. She refused to meet his gaze, keeping hers trained on Chen.

The two detectives exchanged a look, and Halsey took over

again.

"Ms. Miller. Beth, if I may. We aren't here to question you. We're here to warn you."

"About what?" Tom could keep silent no longer. "What the hell is going on?"

"Tom..." Beth laid a cool hand on his arm. It was strange that she was now trying to comfort him when a minute ago he was trying to protect her. From what, he still didn't know.

"Detective, please. Just spit it out." Beth's weariness came through loud and clear. "What do you need to warn me about? It can't have anything to do with Eric. He's in jail."

The detectives' silence spoke volumes.

Beth stood straighter, spoke louder. "Isn't he?"

Her posture demonstrated assertion, but her voice wavered. Damn, he wished he knew what was going on here!

"Beth, I hate to tell you this, but Eric Sharpe is not in jail at this time." Halsey's voice gentled even as he delivered the worst news of all.

"He escaped custody en route from the county jail to the state prison. And based upon the threats he shouted in the courtroom, we think he's coming after you."

Chapter Seven

Beth still couldn't believe what the police detectives had told her.

They'd left thirty minutes ago, and she remained in a state of semi-shock. Eric was free and may be after her? She doubted it.

Detective Chen had explained how the San Francisco PD had tracked her down through her father and the record company. When officials contacted Freestone Records, they were informed of the tour schedule. The Baltimore PD was then put in charge of finding Beth and warning her of possible danger.

"Feeling any better?" Tom's soothing southern drawl washed over her, warming Beth from the outside in. He hadn't left her side from the moment the detectives had arrived.

They sat in the same seats they'd occupied earlier, yet everything had changed. There was no going back to the relatively carefree banter they'd had before.

Tom hadn't said a word about what had transpired, but Beth knew she owed him an explanation. She just didn't know how to begin.

"I'm doing okay," she finally answered. "Thanks." The words weren't exactly true, but, for some reason, she wanted to reassure Tom. He was so concerned about her that she worried about him!

But no matter how much she cared for Tom, she couldn't force him to return the feeling. And he wouldn't. After Beth told him the truth about Eric and what happened in San Francisco, any tender thoughts he harbored for her at the moment would definitely disappear. No sane man would want anything to do with her after knowing all that.

And Tom was definitely sane.

A little annoying at times, but definitely sane.

With his career on the rise, he wouldn't want even a short fling with her. Her bad history was not a selling point.

But he deserved to know it, regardless of the consequences. And no matter how irritated Tom had made her feel earlier, there was now a heaviness in her heart.

Convinced their relationship was over before it had really begun, Beth turned to face him.

•

Tom waited patiently for Beth to speak. Finally she said, "I suppose you want me to explain all of that to you."

Inside, Tom shouted Hell, yes!

But realistically he knew Beth needed to divulge things at her own pace. So he restrained himself and spoke calmly.

"You don't have to explain anything to me. But if you need to talk about it, I'll listen."

And, slowly, she began to tell her story.

"I think I already told you I was on the road with my dad until I turned eighteen. That year I was accepted to Stanford. I worked my butt off and earned my MBA in five years instead of six."

"My years in college—and before that, on the road—weren't very conducive to forming lasting relationships. Of any kind." She glanced up at him, obviously trying to determine if he got her message.

Yeah, he understood. No boyfriends or lovers until after college.

Got it.

"So …" She cleared her throat. "I had an internship at a really prestigious accounting firm, and they liked me so much they offered me a job right out of school."

Beth looked him in the eye, unblinking. "Eric worked at that firm."

All right. Now they were getting down to the nitty-gritty.

Maybe.

Tom prodded carefully when silence lengthened and it appeared Beth's resolution was fading. "What happened with this Eric guy?"

She took a deep breath, let it out slowly.

"You know that saying about office romances never working out?" The rhetorical question needed no reply, so Beth continued on. "Well, I learned it the hard way."

She settled more comfortably in the padded seat, seemingly

preparing to tell a long, heart-wrenching tale.

"I was hired as a junior accountant. Eric was my immediate supervisor, a senior accountant. He was handsome, charming, and hardworking."

Tom didn't like him based on that statement alone.

"Eric had been at the company for almost fifteen years, and he wanted badly to make partner."

Beth gave him an embarrassed look. "Yeah, he was a lot older. And I admit I was bowled over by all the attention he gave me. At first I thought he was just being nice. Trying to show me the ropes since I was new to the firm and the industry in general. But then things changed."

Uh, oh. Tom knew he wasn't going to like this.

"After working there about six months, I was staying late one night. I didn't think anyone else in my section had stayed, but it turns out Eric was still in his office. On his way out he noticed I was at my desk. He suggested we have dinner together, and I agreed."

Now Beth looked completely away from him, gazing blindly toward the stage. What was she so ashamed of?

"From there things happened really fast. Like I said, I was bowled over. Eric and I had dinner together almost every night for the next three weeks. By the end of that time, we'd ended up in bed."

Still she refused to look at him.

"Eric said he cared for me, but we had to keep our relationship secret at the office. Company rules and all that." She shrugged a shoulder. "I believed him." Beth finally turned to meet his gaze, her blue eyes full of pain. "I believed him about a lot of things."

He couldn't take this much longer. Tom reached out to take Beth's hand, hoping to give comfort and at the same time encourage her to continue talking.

"What did he do to you?"

Another heavy sigh escaped her, but Bethany didn't remove her hand from his grasp. If anything, she seemed to hold on even tighter.

"We were lovers for nearly a year. I thought our relationship was really going somewhere. Especially after I got a promotion and we had more or less equal responsibilities. Technically Eric remained my supervisor, but I'd been given some different projects to handle. A couple small firms and one huge one. JCM, Inc., a hot new cyber-technology firm. It was a multi-million dollar account which, I guess, was supposed to be my ultimate training ground."

Tom presumed it hadn't exactly worked out that way.

"I took care of the company's books, but Eric had to double-check everything I did. It really should have irritated him to do that, seeing as he still had his own accounts to manage, but he never complained." A crooked smile briefly broke across her face. "It turns out he was happy with the extra duties."

It was just enough of a comment to lead Tom on. "Why?"

"Because he could learn how I set up my accounts. How I arranged my files—both electronic and hard copies. Where and how to access those files."

Crap.

He hoped this wasn't heading where he thought it was.

Tom tried to feel his way along. "So Eric somehow mismanaged money in your accounts and you got in trouble for it?"

An unladylike snort was Beth's reply to that stupid comment.

"I really don't think the term mismanagement applies when it involves 1.5 million dollars."

Oh.

Double crap.

Beth's face tightened with anger, an emotion Tom was happy to finally see in her. "The appropriate term is embezzlement. At least, that's what the SFPD told me when I was arrested."

Her voice got harder as she continued. "It seems Eric, my trustworthy lover, my supposed soul mate, didn't care for me at all. He only got close to me so he could frame me. He got access to all my files, anything at the office or at home. He probably figured out my computer passwords from personal information I shared. Or maybe I just told him outright. Who knows…I was gullible enough to trust him with other things, so why not security codes, too?"

Tom lifted her hand for a soft kiss, then placed it on his thigh. "You did nothing wrong. He did."

Beth gave him a disbelieving look. "Well, the police and my bosses didn't see it that way. Eric had manipulated the books in a way that implicated me but not him. He reviewed my work on the account, then he'd generate a report for his superiors. What I didn't know was that he was modifying my numbers before he sent in his monthly reports. When the discrepancies between our books and JCM's were finally caught, it all came back to me."

"I was shown the reports Eric had sent, and I knew something was wrong. The numbers didn't look right to me. But when I checked my work files, the numbers matched what was in the reports. The police had their proof, and I had given it to them."

Tom could literally feel Beth's distress as her short fingernails dug into his thigh. They'd leave a mark even through his jeans.

"I knew right then that Eric had done it. He was the only one who could have. I didn't care where I was or who saw me. I was in handcuffs, in police custody, in full view of all my co-workers. And I screamed at him."

"'How could you do this to me? You said you loved me! Why did you do this?' It didn't matter what I yelled. He never even looked at me. He just spoke to the police."

Bethany tugged her hand away, pulled her knees to her chest and wrapped her arms around herself as if she were cold. She spoke softly, carefully, staring off into space again.

"That bastard denied that we were in a relationship. He claimed I tried many times to seduce him, maybe to get him to go along with my embezzling plans." Even in profile, Tom saw her eyes narrow.

"I was humiliated. He painted me as a love-starved psycho as well as a thief."

He could stand it no more. Tom dragged Bethany onto his lap and into his arms, placed gentle kisses along her hairline.

"But you're here now, sweetheart." Another tender kiss, this time on her full lips. "So how did you get cleared?"

Beth's hand gripped his shirt, pressed warm against his chest. She gave a quick smile, and a look of satisfaction flashed in her expressive eyes. "Eric didn't know everything, thank God."

"I backed up my files on a CD each month before I sent them to him. It was a habit I acquired in college, and, luckily, I never broke myself of it."

"And the forensics lab found Eric's fingerprints at my apartment. He tried to blow it off by saying he'd driven me home after work one night, when my car was in the shop." Beth tucked her head under his chin. "But that explanation didn't fly since they found his prints not only by the door but also on the headboard of my bed. Other private places, too. He couldn't deny our relationship after that."

Tom stroked his hands up and down Beth's back, knowing this wasn't easy for her to share. She let out another deep sigh, causing a firm breast to press into his chest.

"Eric wasn't able to change the computer's record of when he altered my files, so the crime lab didn't have to work too hard to find that evidence. And since my CD copies of the original files also had a computer date stamp, the police really had all the proof they needed to charge him. They released me within a few days, but the trial dragged on for a while. It was a nightmare."

Tom remembered what Detective Halsey had said earlier, and rage flowed through him. Bethany had gotten emotionally jerked around, framed for embezzlement, and then had to relive it all when she testified in court. Sharpe's threats were acidic icing on an already poisonous cake.

"What did that bastard say to you? What did he threaten to do?"

Beth lifted her head. Her gaze traveled over his face as her fingers caressed his clenched jaw. "Don't worry about it. He called me nasty names, said he was going to get me for this. You know— the usual bluster of a raving lunatic."

Her eyes met his. With all her anger melted away, there was nothing left but a calm, clear sea of pale blue.

"I don't believe Eric would ever waste his time coming after me. He was caught mostly due to his own carelessness. I really contributed only a small part to the evidence."

"How can you say that? You gave the cops your back-up files. You let them search through all your personal stuff to get his prints, proving he was a liar and had access to your work outside the office. I'd say that was a lot!"

Tom couldn't believe she wasn't concerned for her own welfare. But that was okay. He'd worry enough for the both of them.

And he would make sure Bethany stayed safe.

Chapter Eight

Beth could tell Tom didn't believe her. She appreciated the anger and concern she saw in his dark brown eyes, but she didn't think it was necessary. Eric would only be focused on staying out of prison—not exacting revenge on her.

No, she didn't want Tom thinking about the past, per se. She was only interested in whether he still wanted a relationship with her despite her past.

She supposed this was the time to find out for sure, now that all her naïveté—or was that stupidity?—was out in the open.

"So … do you think you could find an idiot like me attractive? I mean, how much did that story turn you off?"

Beth lost her nerve, dropping her gaze to where her hand rested against his warm, strong chest. She could feel his heart beating steadily beneath her palm, and she hoped she'd soon have the chance to caress his bare skin at leisure.

Tom would have none of her reticence. He lifted her chin, staring hard into her eyes before slowly moving forward to press a long, lingering kiss on her lips. Her mouth opened beneath his, and his tongue hungrily explored inside.

After what seemed like an endless amount of time, he pulled back, breathing harshly. Beth could only stare at him, disorientated.

"I hope that answers your question. But in case my actions weren't clear, here are the words." The intensity of his gaze held her in place. "What happened to you in San Francisco does not make you an idiot. It doesn't make you stupid or dishonest or promiscuous, either." He paused. "It makes you human."

Beth forcibly cleared her mind so she could focus on what he was saying to her.

"Did you do anything wrong? Anything criminal?"

She shook her head. "No, but—"

"Did you do anything wrong?" Tom asked again, more insistently.

"No. I didn't take any money."

He cupped her face in his hands. Spoke softly, but firmly. "Then why would I treat you any different than I did before? Why would I feel any different?"

She absorbed the care and acceptance emanating from him. His reaction to her story floored her, and she fought against the unexpected moisture welling in her eyes.

"The only thing you did was have a lapse in judgment. You got involved with someone, and it turned out bad."

She couldn't help but give him a look. Oh, please.

"Fine. It turned out really bad," he conceded. "But, in my opinion, that still doesn't reflect poorly on you. We all have relationships which don't work out, one way or another, before we find the right person."

Wait, was Tom hinting that he was the right person for her?

She certainly hoped not. She couldn't, and wouldn't, go through another disastrous relationship.

Eric had hurt her on purpose, meaning to send her off to prison while he walked away scot-free.

Tom would hurt her, too. He wouldn't mean to do it. She knew he was a good man, that he cared about her.

But she also knew his planned path in life led in the opposite direction from hers.

Heartbreak was inevitable in the long run, which was why she couldn't allow herself to care too deeply for the man.

Right, she told herself as Tom leaned down to give her another soft, tender kiss.

Like she wasn't already way past that point.

•

"Guys, I've got good news!"

As George entered the room, Tom turned toward him, expecting to hear a second line relating to car insurance.

But George waited until he had the attention of everybody in the backstage dressing area.

"I just got off the phone with Marty. Freestone is very impressed with what's happened on tour so far. The shows have all sold out.

More merchandise had to be ordered because we ran out in Richmond. The CD is getting serious radio play, and it's moving up the charts quick."

"Yeah, George, that's great news," Leo said.

The rest of Roadhouse nodded in agreement, backslaps and congratulatory comments flying among the men.

"But that's not all. There's more to it." George again waited for silence. "You're being upgraded to a tour bus as of tonight. No more motor homes."

Tom thought of Beth. "What about the crew?"

The older man knew what was on his mind. Or rather, who. "Beth will be fine. She'll be on a second bus with me and the other guys. Hotel rooms have been reserved for you for the remainder of the tour. They'll be within walking distance or maybe a short drive away from the concert halls."

George waved and turned to leave. "No dawdling after the show tonight, boys. You've got packing to do."

Despite Tom needing to complete his preparations to go on stage, he hurried to catch up with George as the man crossed into the backstage hallway.

"George?"

The road manager turned, an inquisitive look on his face.

"Yes, Tom?"

"I need to talk to you. About Beth."

George's eyes flicked past Tom's shoulder. He turned to see his band mates unabashedly looking his way, listening in on his conversation.

Tom loved the guys like brothers, but he didn't want any stories circulating about Beth that she herself didn't tell in the first place.

He reached out and pulled the dressing room door firmly shut. "Sorry, fellows."

He turned to George once again, ignoring the "Oh, man!" and other sounds of frustration at his back.

"What's up, Tom?"

He hesitated, unsure of what exactly Bethany had told her father about the police visit earlier that day. Or if she'd told him anything at all.

But fear for her safety was foremost in his mind, and he was willing to share her secret with the only family she had if it meant she'd be better protected.

"Did Beth tell you what happened earlier, during her break?"

George's cheery disposition instantly disappeared. "I know the police were here, and that Eric Sharpe is running around free, possibly intending to hurt my daughter. I assume that's what you're referring to?"

"Yeah, that's it exactly." Tom was happy Beth hadn't kept the news from her father. He felt better knowing he had help in looking out for her. "I'm real glad to hear about the bus situation. Especially now. If Beth still had to stay with Hannah and Liz in their motor home alone, with no real protection, I'd go nuts. This change couldn't have come at a better time."

"Tom, don't worry so much. If that creep ever tries to come near Beth, he'll have to get through me and the rest of the crew first. All the concert halls have top-notch security, and the hotels do, too."

"But to be on the safe side," George continued, "I'll get a picture of Sharpe faxed to the scheduled venues, to put them on watch ahead of time. If he shows up, the cops will get 'em."

Understanding radiated from the man's blue eyes. They were a shade darker than his daughter's, but just as expressive. After a short hesitation, he went on in a softer tone.

"I know you care for my daughter. And I know she cares for you, too. I've seen how you two look at each other. Hell, anyone who's been in the same room as you guys has seen it."

"But don't let those feelings get in the way of the music. You won't get this opportunity again. There are plenty of bands waiting to take Roadhouse's place."

George placed a hand on Tom's shoulder. Gave it a quick, firm shake. "Don't get me wrong. I'd be damn glad to have you as my son-in-law. But I've been in this business longer than you've been alive. I don't want to see you regret that you didn't give this your best shot when you had the chance."

George's gaze narrowed. His grip hardened.

"And if you're not happy with yourself, there's no way you could be making my little girl happy."

He gave Tom's shoulder one final pat before removing his hand. "The tour is over in three weeks. Bethany will still be around when it's over. Trust me."

"She'll be safe, and she'll be there for you. No matter how things go in your career, she'll still be there."

And with that, George resumed his retreat to the stage area, leaving Tom to ponder the man's prophetic remarks.

•

After her first "date" with Tom in Macon, Beth had deliberately stayed nearby to watch each Roadhouse performance. Technically she was off-duty during the shows, but she loved watching them. It didn't matter that she had to get right back to work afterward, disassembling and packing up equipment. She couldn't not watch.

And it wasn't just Tom that held her attention. The dynamics of the group, how they interacted with each other and with the audience, held her enthralled.

The length of the performance was twice that of the average band's set. Not having an opening act gave more time for Roadhouse to showcase their talents. But since they'd only released one album, they had a limited number of original songs to play.

And no matter how popular those songs were, nobody wanted to hear them three times in the same night.

So Roadhouse interspersed their own songs with cover versions of hits from other bands. They put their distinctive spin on tunes from the Beatles to the Stones and Eagles, from Motown harmonies to *a cappella* ditties.

No genre of music was exempt from their brand of attention. And no matter what they played, they kept the audience, including Beth, enraptured.

It wasn't just the songs they sang; it was their incredible energy. They frequently changed instruments, showing their versatilities not only in song styles but also in abilities.

Electric guitars gave way to acoustic ones. A drum set gave way to bongos. Electric keyboards gave way to a grand piano. The guys utilized solos to highlight their talents, regardless of which instrument they were playing at the time.

Even Liz and Hannah added to the melodies being played by occasionally banging and shaking tambourines.

Through it all, Beth could see how much fun everyone was having, how overwhelming the whole experience was. Especially during slow ballads, she could see the intense emotions on the guys' faces.

And no matter how sad the lyrics of the song were, she knew the members of Roadhouse wouldn't trade that moment, on that stage, for anything else in the world.

Her current viewpoint from near the speaker tower at stage right allowed her to see both the band and the first rows of the audience. The fans were swaying in their seats, singing and clapping along to the rocking beat of one of Roadhouse's own country tunes.

As her gaze traveled over the excited crowd, something struck her as odd.

Beth's eyes sought out and found what had seemed out of place—a younger, dark-haired woman sitting a few rows back. She was just sitting there, staring at the stage.

While everyone around her was enjoying the performance, smiling, laughing, moving with the music, this girl just sat still, seemingly immune to the activities around her.

Maybe she was deaf, although it would've been pretty stupid to spend money for a concert she couldn't hear.

She could be blind, but she'd still be able to hear the music and react to it, which wasn't happening.

And Beth could see the brunette's head moving, following the movements of someone on stage. She shifted her own gaze.

It was Tom.

The fan was watching Tom as he crossed the stage, performing a rousing solo near the end of the song.

Yeah, the man could play.

The muscles in his forearms flexed and shifted as he put everything he had into the music. His grin was blinding.

As Beth's focus narrowed on Tom, a final thought of the too-serious spectator ran through her mind.

Maybe the girl hadn't cared much for that particular song …

•

She was thrilled.

It was much easier to follow a bright red bus on the highway than a string of motor homes. Especially since it was vacation season and it seemed like every other vehicle she passed was a camper of some sort.

She was definitely making a huge leap in her progress to make Tom Crowley hers forever.

She'd be able to secure a room at the same places Roadhouse

stayed. No more hanging out in parking lots, trying to glimpse her man through chain-link fences. And no more standing around on street corners, giving the impression she was a prostitute on the lookout for a john. That was so far from the truth it was laughable. She was unequivocally a one-man woman.

It was about time that management appreciated how hard Tom and his friends were working. The band should've been treated to plush tour buses and fine hotels way before now.

She'd been afraid she was going to have to call in some favors to change things. She hadn't wanted to exert any influence over Tom's career—she knew he had the talent to succeed on his own—but she was willing to do whatever it took to help him.

Even if it meant exposing her feelings too soon by engaging in a power play with his production company.

Good thing it hadn't come to that in the end.

She really wanted to surprise Tom gently, show her devotion to him in a tender way.

She didn't have all the specifics planned out yet, but the general course of action was clear in her head.

And staying in the same hotels as her true love was going to make his seduction flow that much smoother.

Chapter Nine

Tom was feeling good.

Aside from the fact Bethany wasn't in his sight, things were going well.

The tour bus he was currently riding in was a hell of a lot more comfortable than the band's prior travel accommodations, and he really felt like Roadhouse was going someplace now. Other than Reading, Pennsylvania, that is.

He felt they were finally being recognized as more than a one-hit-wonder, fly-by-night band. He was proud. And happy.

And the only thing that would make him happier at this moment would be if Beth were sitting beside him. Safe.

Logically, he knew she couldn't be any better protected than she was right now. She was ensconced in a moving vehicle with ten able-bodied men—including her father—keeping her company. There was no way Eric Sharpe could get to her.

So he had to admit to himself that the real reason he wanted Beth here was because he missed her.

Even though he had plenty of people he could converse with, he wanted to hear Beth's voice.

Tom let his gaze roam around the bus, taking in Leo and Jack catching a few ZZZs in large reclining seats, and Dylan and Sam passing the time with a leisurely game of cards.

Liz and Hannah sat closest to him, engaged in a quiet but animated conversation.

He studied them, noting they were both long-legged, with trim, athletic builds. But where Liz had long, wavy, near-black hair, Hannah sported a copper-colored chin-length 'do.

They were attractive women, but neither one of them stirred his senses, his heart, the way Bethany did.

Just then Hannah glanced his way and caught his gaze. He gave her a quick smile, not knowing how weak it looked, or how forlorn he appeared.

Hannah spoke briefly to Liz, who nodded in response and pulled a paperback out of her oversized purse. As Liz immersed herself in her book, Hannah came over to Tom.

"Hey, are you doing okay?" She folded a leg beneath her, gracefully dropping onto the sofa beside him. She propped her elbow on the back of the sofa and leaned her head into her hand. It was a casual pose, but her green eyes showed concern. "You don't look too happy right now. Don't you think the show went well?"

"No, that's not it. Everything's going great."

Hannah's face softened, and she gave a teasing smile. "So it's Beth then? She's what's making you pout like a two-year-old who's not allowed to play with his favorite toy?"

Her analogy made him laugh, but he still wanted to be cautious about how much of Beth's history he told.

"I'm worried about her."

All kidding disappeared from Hannah's face. "Yeah. She told us about this Eric creep. She wanted us to be on the lookout for him. Not for her own sake, but for ours. Beth said it wasn't likely he'd show up, but she wanted us to be careful, just in case."

Tom sighed and let his head drop back onto the sofa cushion. "That woman is driving me crazy. She won't take this threat seriously. She's more worried about everyone else than she is about herself."

He turned his head to look at Hannah. "If anything happens to her, I'll lose it. I know I haven't known her that long, but I really care about her."

Hannah reached out to give a couple friendly pats to his arm. "Love is ignorant of time. You can't choose when it hits, or how long it will last. You just enjoy it while it's there."

He wasn't sure how to reply. He didn't know if what he felt for Beth was love or not.

And if it was love, he wanted Bethany to be the first one he acknowledged it to.

Hannah seemed to understand he needed to think on what she'd said, so she changed the subject. Sort of.

"I like Beth, too. She's fun, and smart, and she sings great, too."

Now that was news to Tom.

He loved the sound of Beth's speaking voice, but just because a person spoke well didn't mean he or she could sing well, and vice versa. He was intrigued.

"How do you know that?"

Hannah rolled her eyes at him. "I didn't listen to her singing in the shower, if that's what you're thinking."

The imagery her comment conjured up was enough to severely distract Tom.

Beth, in the shower, with water streaming over her body.

The graceful curve of her neck exposed as she leaned into the spray to wet and then lather her thick strands of blonde hair.

Her hands leisurely soaping up every curve and crevice, lingering a bit more in certain sensitive places.

The cascade of water rinsing all the soap bubbles from her skin, with small droplets clinging precariously to protruding areas.

Like her long eyelashes … her pert nose.

Her pale pink nipples.

Tom shifted uncomfortably, hoping that Hannah's sharp gaze didn't drop to his lap.

How embarrassing. And pathetic.

He was hard at just the thought of Bethany naked in the shower.

If he found the simple task of her bathing to be erotic, he was afraid to think about her in more outright sexual situations. Like making love with him.

In various positions, various locations.

His groin tightened even more, threatening to cut off his very breath.

He had to refocus his mind, and fast.

Now, what had they been talking about? Oh, yeah. Beth's singing ability.

"So, how do you know she can sing?" Tom asked as casually as possible. He strived to appear relaxed, and not horny as a thirteen-year-old looking at his first *Playboy*.

Thankfully Hannah's eyes stayed on his face, but a quick twitch of her lips betrayed her thoughts.

She knew where his mind had gone, damn it. And she'd probably led him in that direction on purpose.

Women. He loved 'em, but he'd never understand 'em.

"The answer to that question," the redheaded witch explained, "is that Beth liked to rehearse with us. Nothing formal, but she'd sing along as we practiced our parts. Sometimes she'd do some of the dance moves, too."

Admiration gleamed in her eyes. "Like I said, Beth is sharp. She's got good range, reads music, and she has the lyrics of the entire set memorized. Not just backing, but the lead vocals, too. Better watch out or she'll be learning to play guitar next."

Well this was definitely something he wanted to talk to Bethany about.

She'd given him the impression that working as a roadie was dead last on her list of job choices. That she was only here because she'd had few options available after the embezzling fiasco.

And she'd claimed when they'd first met that she didn't even like country music.

So why was it that she was spending precious free time immersed in a musician-esque lifestyle?

Perhaps her tastes had changed over the course of the tour, or maybe she just enjoyed interacting with Liz and Hannah.

But why not be up front with him? Why hide the fact that she liked his music, and, in fact, liked to sing?

Was this another thing she was ashamed of for some unknown reason?

He was getting a headache. Trying to discern what went on in Bethany's head was exhausting. Odds were he would never fully understand her, even if he spent the rest of his life trying to figure her out.

But maybe that wasn't such a bad thing.

•

Beth wasn't sure what to do.

They were near the halfway point in Roadhouse's tour, and in less than three weeks she'd be saying goodbye to Tom.

She didn't want to.

Really, really didn't want to.

But she knew it had to be done. For both their sakes.

And since they were running out of time rather quickly, it was doubtful they'd even get the chance to make love before they parted ways.

She would've loved to carry that memory with her, but it seemed it wasn't meant to be.

Beth shifted restlessly in the padded bus seat. She knew she should be using this opportunity to sleep, but even as she forced her eyes closed, her mind refused to shut down.

It wasn't Eric Sharpe that kept her awake—she really wasn't worried that he'd show up in her vicinity.

No, Tom Crowley was the one she couldn't evict from her thoughts.

She remembered how he'd been at dinner in Macon. Inquisitive, attentive. Sweet.

Then later, playing mini golf. He'd appeared relaxed but had shown a slight competitive streak, too.

And she saw him as he'd appeared a few hours ago on stage. Hot. Sweaty. Full of energy.

As her brain began to wind down after a long day, those images intertwined and became her ultimate fantasy of late.

Tom stood in front of her as she lay naked on the bed. He'd removed his shirt—or maybe she had done it—but still wore jeans.

Which were unbuttoned and halfway unzipped at his trim waist, baring the trail of crisp, dark hair beneath his navel. They were barely hanging on to his narrow hips.

Teasing her.

Tempting her.

She stretched out a hand to pull the offending piece of clothing down, but he shook his head and moved back, out of her reach.

"Not yet," was all he said.

And he continued to look at her. All of her.

She forced her arm back to her side, her whole body quivering from the intense heat shining in his eyes.

She felt exposed, but energized. This was what she'd been waiting for. To experience Tom, and all he had to offer, in the most intimate ways possible.

"Turn over."

She followed his command without question, using folded arms to cushion her head.

She wasn't afraid. In fact, she was eager to experience whatever pleasures he had in mind for her.

And then she intended to return the favor.

She jumped at the unexpected touch of his callused fingers on her shoulders. But as the roughened texture of his skin slid over the smoothness of hers, she quickly relaxed again.

Relatively speaking.

She felt the mattress give as Tom moved to straddle her bottom, still massaging her shoulders. Then he pushed her hair to the side, leaned down to press gentle kisses against the sensitive nape of her neck. His denim-encased erection cradled snugly against her backside, shifting with his movements.

She was melting.

Anyone looking for her in the morning would find only a big puddle where she now lay.

This was better than she'd dreamed it would be, and he'd hardly touched her.

He slowly slid down her body, meticulously caressing, kissing, and licking every inch of her skin.

She ached inside, wanting more. Wanting to see him and touch him, the way he was touching her.

At last he reached her toes. She'd never before thought her feet were sexy, but he seemed fascinated by them. He massaged them with his strong hands, then bent her knees up and sucked her toes with his equally strong mouth.

Then it was time.

"Turn back over."

She didn't know how she summoned the strength, but she did it.

Again she reached to tug his jeans down and again he pulled away.

"I'm not through yet."

He moved to sit astride her once more, but hesitated.

"All of you looks so delicious, I'm not sure where to start." His dark eyes gleamed with mischief, toying with her. "What do you think? Where should I begin, top or bottom?"

He wasn't going to make a move unless she answered him.

It seemed that her whole being yearned for his touch. Her tingling breasts and the warm area between her thighs begged for attention. But even more important than that, she wanted a kiss.

A simple, tender touch of his lips against hers. A caring gesture which demonstrated how deeply affected he was by this act—the act of lovemaking.

Which was what she was. In love.

With Tom.

And she wanted to show him that love the only way she knew how.

"Top," she said breathlessly.

He didn't move to straddle her again, but instead sat by her side. He leaned over her, his muscular arms supporting most of his weight, caging her in. His firm chest seared her where it pressed against her taut nipples. Her arms were pinned to her side, her hands unable to caress him.

For the longest time they just stared into each other's eyes. She hoped he, too, was realizing how significant this moment truly was.

Overwhelmed at the feelings burgeoning inside her, Beth's eyes slowly closed.

And he leaned down to brush his lips against hers. So softly that she almost believed it hadn't happened.

But then he did it again. Letting his mouth linger a little longer this time, but pressing no harder.

She strained to free her arms, needing to pull him closer, hold him longer. But he wouldn't allow it.

"Beth," he murmured, shifting to place kisses on her cheeks, her forehead.

"Beth, come on," he urged softly.

Come on, what? He wouldn't let her do anything.

She tried once more to move her arms, but it wasn't happening. They were firmly held in place.

"Come on." Another soft kiss on her lips. "Time to get up, sleepyhead."

What?

She forced her heavy eyelids open. Blinked a few times to clear her vision.

But instead of seeing Tom half naked and sitting beside her, he was fully clothed and kneeling in front of her.

She was slumped in a seat of the tour bus she'd boarded last night after the concert. Like Tom she was fully clothed, but she was pretty sure his underpants weren't soaking wet like hers were.

What a dream.

If Tom hadn't grasped her upper arms and awakened her with soft words and softer kisses, she probably would have embarrassed herself with a loud, powerful orgasm.

And that wasn't how she wanted to greet her co-workers in the morning. She was uncomfortable enough as it was, with Tom hovering over her in front of everybody.

Beth took a quick look around, only then noticing that no one else remained on the bus. It was just her and Tom.

Well, at least she only had one person to face after that hot fantasy.

Except that person happened to be the star of her wet dream, and facing him wasn't going to be easy.

She licked her dry lips, cleared her throat. Focused on his mouth, still too flustered to meet his gaze.

Big mistake.

His attractive mouth was what had gotten her in this condition in the first place.

She quickly but unsteadily pushed to her feet, shaking off his hold. Tom was forced to stand and move out of her way.

"So, where is everybody?" Beth turned, ostensibly to look out the bus window, but really so she could scrub the sleepiness, and arousal, from her face.

"It's around six AM. We're at a diner not far from the hotel. Everyone's in having breakfast."

She turned back to him, a bright smile plastered on her face. "Great! Let's go. I'm starved!"

"Um, Beth? You might want to freshen up before we go in."

Beth instantly looked down, afraid he'd seen residual signs of her desire. But everything looked pretty normal to her. Her nipples had softened, and the dampness between her legs hadn't left any telltale spot on her jeans.

She looked up and saw Tom's gaze focused on her hair.

She raised her hands and found that the thick ponytail she'd had last night no longer existed. Her hair was hanging loose, in a wild, tangled disarray around her face.

Oh, God.

Had she done that while she'd slept? While she'd dreamt of Tom?

She prayed no one on the bus had witnessed her actions. Lord knew where else her hands had traveled during the night.

Embarrassment returned full force. She had to escape and pull herself together.

"Excuse me," she mumbled as she snatched her carry-on from the seat and pushed past Tom, heading for the bathroom at the rear of the bus. "I'll be right back."

"I'll be waiting," was his reply.

And he was.

When she emerged from the small rest room a few minutes later, her bladder empty, clothes changed, face washed, teeth brushed, and hair once again neatly pulled back—this time with a large clip—Tom was seated near the bus door, flipping through a magazine.

He looked up and smiled as she came toward him. Her heart flip-flopped, and as he rose and extended his hand to her, she remembered.

In her fantasy, she'd admitted to herself that she loved him. That's why she'd wanted so badly to make love with him.

They exited the bus in silence. Tom lifted her hand to plant a habitual kiss on her knuckles, but he didn't miss a step as he led her toward the diner.

Good thing he was a good leader, because if left to her own devices, she wouldn't have a clue what she was doing.

She was numb.

Scared.

Because although the physical intimacies she'd experienced last night had been figments of her imagination, the emotions they'd evoked were all too real.

She was in love with Tom. Deeply in love.

This wasn't the half-ass emotion she'd felt for Eric prior to her arrest. No infatuation here—this was the real deal.

And she didn't think it was going away any time soon.

•

Tom held the door open for Bethany and allowed her to precede him into the diner. He was hungry as a horse, as the saying goes.

Once Hannah had left him alone last night, he'd dozed off, guided by images of the woman by his side.

He didn't remember any details of what he'd dreamt, but he'd woke with a smile on his face and a ravenous feeling in his gut. The kind of feeling a man gets after a period of strenuous exercise.

He only wished the kind of exercise he'd imagined had been reality.

But there was always later, at the hotel. He was sure he could find time alone with Beth at some point today. They actually had an extra day off scheduled this week, leaving plenty of time for socializing.

Maybe they could finally make some of his dreams come true. But right now, he was hoping to just sit next to her while they had breakfast.

"Hey, Beth! Over here!" Cole's loud, eager voice interrupted Tom's musings. "We saved a seat for you."

So much for that little wish.

"Go ahead," he told Beth. "I'll catch up with you later."

He watched as she gave her father a good morning kiss and sat down beside him, then Tom moved to a nearby table where Leo was seated.

At least he wouldn't have to crane his neck to look at her. From this vantage point, he could see Beth's face clearly as she spoke with Mike, Cole, and George. It was a poor consolation prize, but he'd take it.

The waitress came to take their orders, and a short while later the band and crew were served dishes overflowing with hot food. Conversation slowed and eventually stopped altogether as people focused on clearing their plates.

It wasn't until meals had been devoured and everyone was lingering over coffee that a comment spoken at Beth's table caught his attention.

"Hey, Beth, you must've been having some nightmare last night. You was squirming around so hard in your seat I figured you was gonna end up on the floor!" It was Cole again, speaking loud enough for half the restaurant to hear.

Tom's eyes shot to Bethany.

Her face was beet red, her eyes open wide as her gaze locked with his.

Then she glanced away, back toward Cole, and began babbling an answer. "Um, yeah. Yeah. It was a horrible nightmare. From childhood."

She darted another glance at Tom, who hadn't bothered to look away.

"My mother died, you know. In a horrible accident. Drunk driver. I was only eight."

Another quick look at Tom.

"That's when I started traveling with Dad, on the road. The motion of the bus probably brought in all out of my subconscious."

It was such an obvious line of bull that Tom almost laughed.

But he couldn't laugh because the fear he'd felt for Beth yesterday came rushing back with full force. It was clear to him that Beth hadn't been dreaming of her dead mother at all.

She'd been dreaming of Eric Sharpe.

She'd put on a good act for him, he'd give her that. He'd honestly believed that she wasn't concerned about Sharpe coming after her.

But she'd just buried the fear, only permitting it to surface while she slept.

Dreams were usually a good place to find hidden truths.

"Tom! Leo!"

The men simultaneously turned to see what was happening.

Liz rushed toward them, her naturally olive complexion now pale and streaked with silent tears, cell phone clutched in hand. Hannah, Dylan, Sam, and Jack were close behind her.

"I have to leave! I have to go home!"

"What's going on?" Leo asked.

"My mother's had a stroke. I have to get home—there's no one else!"

The women had been singing with Roadhouse for a couple years, so Tom was aware of Liz's situation. Her elderly mother lived on her own, and Liz's brother was in the Navy, currently somewhere overseas.

He knew how close Liz and her mother were, and he understood that she had to get back to Savannah. He would've done the same thing if his own mother were alive and needed assistance.

Nothing was more important than family.

Tom looked around at the other members of Roadhouse. Their faces showed sympathy, and he knew they all felt as he did.

"Go on, Liz. Head on home. We all wish you the best of luck. Let us know how your mom is doing."

Murmurs of acquiescence and condolence could be heard from the surrounding group.

Hannah wrapped an arm around her friend. "I'll help Liz get her stuff together and make arrangements to get back to Georgia."

Liz started crying again, loudly this time. "I'm so sorry, guys. But I can't stay. I—I just can't."

"Shh. Things will be fine around here." Hannah hugged Liz and gave her a reassuring pat on the back. "The only person you need to worry about is your mother. Now, come on. Let's get you back to her."

Goodbyes were said, but as the two women made their way out of the diner, Dylan spoke the concern that was in everyone's mind.

"Damn. What are we gonna do? We're short a back-up singer and still have a ton of concerts left."

"We have to cancel the rest of the tour." Jack's response nearly incited a riot among the band and crew. Those seated close by had easily overheard Liz's problem. Which, it now appeared, was everyone's problem.

Amidst the confusion, Leo stated another option. "We're only down one person. How hard could it be to find a replacement?"

"Hmph," was Sam's reply to that. "Do you realize how many fruitcakes we'd be surrounded by if we suddenly advertised for a back-up singer? Not to mention that she'd need to be ready to sing in two days. We couldn't ask that of anyone. It's nuts."

"It's the only choice we have," Leo shot back. He looked around. "Unless you all want to head back home right now?"

Band and crew members alike shook their heads. No, they wanted to complete the tour.

And in the silence that fell over the entire crowd, an idea took root in Tom's mind.

"I know who we can ask."

Chapter Ten

"Are you freakin' crazy?"

Beth couldn't comprehend what was going on in Tom's head. He couldn't have said what she thought he did.

"You're asking me to replace Liz as a back-up singer? I've never done anything like that—you have to find someone else!"

"We don't have time to find someone else," he replied calmly. "And I wouldn't be asking you unless there was a good chance you could do it."

"What gives you that idea?" She couldn't believe this conversation was happening, and in the middle of a restaurant which was getting more crowded by the minute.

"Hannah and I talked last night." He left it at that, but she understood.

Her clandestine singing activities had been revealed to him. And since Hannah had previously raved about Beth's talent, she knew what sort of comments had been made to Tom. She had little hope of convincing him that she stunk.

But maybe she could talk the other members of Roadhouse out of this ridiculous idea.

She turned to Leo Harper, Tom's best friend since high school. He was as fair as Tom was dark, with short, curly blonde hair and bright hazel eyes. "Leo, you can't think this will work," she entreated with open arms.

He shrugged his shoulders, arms crossed over his broad chest. "We have to try. If you're willing to help, that is."

She liked the man, but right then his heavy Texas accent grated on her nerves. Sure, put it back on her.

"We need you." Dylan Talbot looked like a gypsy with his wavy, medium-length black hair and equally dark eyes. He was undeniably good looking, but long eyelashes, prominent cheekbones, and a diamond stud sparkling in his left earlobe almost made him look too pretty. Almost.

Right now his exotic appearance didn't hold her attention, but his simple statement did.

"There has to be someone who can do it better than I can. Don't you guys know any singers from around here?" She looked at the remaining band members one by one, hoping for an affirmative response. From anyone.

Jack Fleming answered, but he didn't say what she wanted to hear. "The three of us have been living in Georgia so long we wouldn't know anybody up here who's qualified. According to Tom, you're it." His brown eyes showed sympathy for her situation, but he didn't help it any.

Beth turned from the sandy-haired keyboardist to her last chance. Sam Waters.

Who was, indeed, one tall, cool drink of water.

She'd never seen him without his battered black Stetson, so she was clueless about his hairstyle—it was even possible he didn't require one. Sam did, however, have a dark, neatly trimmed mustache and goatee, and the bassist's deep blue eyes always radiated intelligence and sincerity. He rarely spoke, but when he did, it was with a Joe Friday "Just the facts, Ma'am" attitude.

If there was any other choice available to the group, she knew Sam would come up with it.

"Beth, you're our only hope right now."

Crap. Her last chance for escape went up in flames.

"But," Sam continued, "there's no guarantee we'll like your sound."

And just like that, the fire was gone. She might still be able to squeeze her way out of this.

"What say you do a little audition for us? You and Hannah can run through some of the backing tracks, and we'll see if we like how you two sound together. If we don't think it'll work, we'll do whatever we have to do to get a different replacement. Sound fair?"

Leave it to sensible Sam to find a plan which was acceptable to everyone. The man originally hailed from Arkansas and still retained a faint southern drawl, but he'd also lived in many big cities of the Northeast. He was a superb blend of North and South, and, through experience, he knew the importance of compromise.

There was no way she could back out now without looking like a heartless brat.

Unless …

She turned to her father. "Dad? What do you think?"

Beth figured he really should have the final say. After all, he'd hired her to be a roadie. Taking Liz's place would leave more work for the remaining technicians.

She waited, hoping George would take the decision out of her hands.

"Bethany, the guys will be able to pick up the slack if you want to do this." Nods from the crew echoed his statement. "They're experienced workers, and we've all had to make adjustments in the past, so don't worry about us not being able to hack it this time."

Yikes. Foiled again.

Beth looked back at Roadhouse. The men she'd once thought had juvenile mentalities were waiting for her answer with serious, yet hopeful, expressions on their handsome faces.

She couldn't let them down. She had gained too much respect for them over the past weeks.

And she wanted to keep their respect, too.

"All right," she relented. "I'll audition for you."

As smiles appeared on their faces, Beth pushed on. "But you guys need to be absolutely honest about how I sound. If I'm not at the standard I should be for your shows, tell me."

"Sure."

"No problem."

More quick nods showed acknowledgement of her terms.

They'd readily agreed to be truthful about her talent, or lack thereof, but Beth had a feeling her life was about to change yet again.

•

Five hours later, Roadhouse had a new back-up singer.

The entire entourage had adjourned to their hotel after breakfast. Following check-in and a quick freshening up, Hannah and Beth had joined the band in their suite.

Where Tom was stunned by Bethany's vocal abilities.

She had to have had formal training, because there was no way an I-just-sing-along-to-the-radio type of person could know what she did.

Everything Hannah had said about Beth was true: She could read sheet music, had terrific range, and sang like an angel.

But she also had an innate sense of what sounded good—something which could only come from personal experience.

Bethany's clear voice was nothing like Liz's more earthy, raspy one, and she knew not to try and duplicate Liz's singing style. Instead, she figured out within two songs the right way to blend her voice with Hannah's in perfect harmony.

The resulting sound was slightly different than Hannah and Liz's mix had been, but even a repeat concertgoer wouldn't be able to discern the difference. Tom was able to detect the subtle variation of the backing vocals because he'd been performing music for over half his life.

And because he was listening intently to every note spilling from Bethany's full lips.

"I guess that settles that," Dylan said as the women finished their final song together. "She's in, right, guys?"

Leo, Jack, and Sam all nodded, confirming what Tom had known half an hour ago.

She was good. And she was going to help them salvage the rest of the tour.

Tom absorbed the shell-shocked look on Beth's face.

Okay, maybe this wouldn't be as easy as they'd all thought.

"Beth, could I speak with you? Alone?" His gaze traveled around the suite, searching for a private area to talk.

The bedroom—no, too much temptation in there.

The bathroom—no, that, too, was off limits after his lascivious imaginings of Bethany in the shower.

Leo interrupted his thoughts as they once again began to stray. "Hey, man, no sweat. We're all heading downstairs for lunch anyway. When you're through, come down to the restaurant."

"Thanks, guys. See you in a few." Tom's smile and nod of appreciation included Hannah, who gave a wink and thumbs up to Beth as she left with the men.

A heavy silence followed the closing of the door, leaving Tom and Beth staring at each other as muted traffic noise from the street below filtered in.

The need to assuage the fear he saw on her face overrode his curiosity about her singing.

"Are you all right?"

"Tom, I can't do this!"

Their simultaneous outbursts broke the ice, and they both smiled.

Tom waved a hand toward Beth. "You go first."

"I just don't think I can do this. I want to help, but I'm not sure I can." She plopped down onto a sofa and leaned her head back to stare at the ceiling.

"What's the problem? You've obviously had experience performing." Which she'd neglected to tell him.

He banked down his irritation at that thought and tried once again to focus on her current concerns.

"My only performances were in community chorus events which had audiences of sixty people, tops. I sang in a group of thirty people, not as half a duo."

Hmm. Interesting. He'd like to get back to that story later.

She turned to look at him as he joined her on the sofa. "I don't want to be selfish. Really. But I don't want to make a fool of myself again and ruin your chance at success while I'm at it."

Aha. Back to the Eric Sharpe catastrophe again. Would the woman ever move on with her life?

He hoped so.

He lifted her hand from the cushion, placed a kiss on the palm. Then he laid it on his thigh, gently rubbing her knuckles with his thumb.

"Your voice is amazing. There's no way you could ruin anything for us."

Signs of doubt still remained on her face, and he wanted badly to make them go away.

Recalling George's words of warning that the music had to come first, Tom resigned himself to spending little time alone with Bethany before Roadhouse's next performance.

"Listen, the concert is two nights away. There's plenty of time to rehearse, and we'll run through the set as many times as it takes for you to feel comfortable. You won't be singing in front of a full auditorium, but it's the best we can do."

A small smile appeared, breaking her somber expression.

"Thanks."

"No. Thank you." He raised her hand for another brief kiss. "Believe me, the more you practice, the more familiar you become with the songs, the better you'll feel on stage. You won't even notice the audience is there because you'll be so involved with the music. It's intense."

"Yeah, I've watched you perform. Intense is definitely a word I'd use to describe it."

Another stricken look crossed her face. "Oh, my God! What about my clothing? Assuming I can actually do this, what will I wear?"

His eyes wandered over her tense form. "Relax. You and Liz are about the same size. Hannah is, too, for that matter. I'm sure something in the wardrobe will fit you."

"But—"

"And," he pressed on, "if for some reason nothing suits you, maybe the concierge can recommend a local tailor, or—"

"Or nothing," she now interrupted him. "Don't even think about buying me an outfit. I'll make sure something fits. And I can do any minor alterations myself. I've acquired more than math skills in my life, you know."

A perfect opening for his next comment.

"Yeah. I found out today that you have quite a few hidden talents."

A pink tide slowly rose over her cheeks, but she remained silent.

"Why is it you neglected to tell me you could sing? And that you liked doing it?"

She pulled her hand away and curled up in a corner of the sofa, arms wrapped around her knees.

But he refused to be put off.

Tom moved closer, until her sandaled feet were touching his thigh. She looked at him with pursed lips, her displeasure palpable.

Too bad.

He wanted some answers.

"I really thought we were getting close. Extremely close."

Her eyes lowered at that, but quickly she lifted her gaze, and her chin, to face him again.

"So can you tell me why you kept something so important to both of us a secret? Didn't you think it was something that could bring us even closer?" He held her gaze, willing her to respond.

"Yes! All right? I did think that!"

"And?"

She averted her face, looking toward a mountain landscape hanging on the far wall.

Then it hit him.

She didn't want to get closer to him.

A terrible ache began in his heart. And, just like that, he knew two things for sure.

He was in love with Bethany.

But she obviously wasn't in love with him.

"Do you still want to have sex with me?" he asked point-blank.

Her head snapped back toward him, eyes narrowed. "What does that have to do with my singing?"

"Just answer the question."

She blew out a harsh breath. "Yes, I want to have sex with you. I'm attracted to you, and I care about you."

She leaned forward to press a warm palm against his cheek. He closed his eyes, welcoming her gentle touch.

"Tom, I didn't mean to upset you," she said softly. "But I figured it wasn't information you needed to have since we'd only be seeing each other for a few weeks. How was I to know this situation would come up?"

The ache in his chest intensified.

"So now you know, and I can help the band. What's the big deal?"

Now he was the one who had to pull away.

He pushed off the sofa and paced to the window. "The big deal is you don't trust me."

"What? Of course I trust you. Otherwise, I wouldn't voluntarily be singing in front of thousands of people."

She, too, stood, and he turned to face her.

"This isn't about the band. It's about us." Tom crossed to Beth, grateful they stood almost eye-to-eye with each other. He wanted them to be equals in whatever hackneyed relationship this was. He didn't want to pressure her into anything.

Even though it was killing him.

"I feel like I've had to forcefully extract every bit of information I know about you."

"That's not true! We've talked about personal stuff plenty of times."

"Yeah. Your favorite color, favorite movie—but those aren't the kinds of things I'm talking about. And the only reason you told me about Eric is because the cops showed up." He took another step closer. "I want to know what's really affected you in your life. What made you the fascinating woman you are today." Tom carefully brushed a loose tendril of hair from her face. "Is that too much to ask?"

He could see from the confusion in her eyes that it was.

So he backed off a little, both physically and emotionally. He dropped his hand and returned to the more generic topic of music. "Could you at least tell me how you became such a great singer?"

He waited, hoping she'd share this small part of herself.

•

Beth moved back to the sofa and watched as Tom also sat down again. This time he stayed at the opposite end, his face unreadable.

She loved him so much. She'd never meant to hurt him.

But obviously she had, and she needed to make up for it.

She didn't want their last weeks together to be ruined by her stupid reluctance to open up.

"I never said I hated music. I just hated the lifestyle I had growing up. I wanted a normal life, with a house, and friends, and dinner on the table at six every night."

"Most kids dream of having the vagabond life you had. Meeting famous musicians, traveling all over the country."

"Yeah, well, the grass is always greener and all that." She slouched down into the cushions and propped her legs on the coffee table.

A flash of heat appeared in Tom's eyes as they followed the line of her extended limbs, bare below her denim shorts. Nice to see her brash personality hadn't totally turned him off.

She supposed she could distract him with sex, now that they were finally alone. But he deserved more than that.

And, for that matter, so did she.

If they actually had the chance to make love before she left, she wanted it to last a while. She didn't want to hurry because friends were waiting to have lunch with them.

"Anyway, when I started college, I'd already thought about trying to graduate early. With accounting being such a grueling, methodical major, I wanted to pick a less intensive minor. Something that was relatively easy."

She shrugged. "Music came easy to me. Even though I resented it as a child, I was surrounded by it and couldn't help absorbing it. It became second nature."

"Math and music aren't all that far apart," Tom observed. "You have to grasp the basic concepts of time and measurement to be any kind of musician. Aside from the way you were raised, I can see why someone like yourself would like singing."

She crooked an eyebrow at him.

"You're a problem-solver. And the arrangement of each song— the rhythm, lyrics, instrumentation—it's all a puzzle which has to be pieced together just right to work. To be good."

Beth mulled over what he'd said. "So you attribute my musical abilities to the analytical side of my brain, not the creative side? You think because I'm an accountant, I can't enjoy music just for itself? I have to love it for its mathematical properties?"

Tom closed his eyes and gripped his short hair until his knuckles turned white. "There's that problem-solving tendency again," he muttered. "Has to have a clear-cut answer for everything."

He emitted a deep sigh, lowered his arms, and stared at her. Hard.

Trapped by his chocolate gaze, she waited for his reply.

"No, I don't think that at all. I think you're smart and creative. You're an intelligent, beautiful, sexy bean counter who can do anything she sets her mind to. Including driving me crazy!"

He moved fast, surrounding her with muscular arms planted on the sofa's back and side. "Now stop trying to change the subject."

Despite his stern warning, her lips curved upward. "You think I'm a sexy bean counter?"

His eyes dropped to her mouth. "Yeah," he growled. "I do."

His lips covered hers, and she felt complete for the first time in days. Long days and even longer, restless nights.

She threaded her fingers through his hair, clasped them around his neck to hold him close.

It had been so long since they'd been able to kiss, let alone anything more. She didn't want to waste a single minute.

Beth loved how he kissed. He took his time, outlining every bit of her mouth with his own before exploring deeper with his tongue.

She took her time exploring his mouth, too. He tasted faintly of mint.

Delicious.

Cupping his jaw in her hands, she felt the stubble covering his skin. Apparently he hadn't had time for shaving that morning, but she didn't mind.

The bristles rubbed against the already sensitized nerve endings of her lips and palms, adding to the feelings of desire coursing through her.

God, she wanted him.

Loved him.

Trusted him. With her entire being.

And that realization made her pull back.

He groaned, leaned in for another kiss. And she couldn't resist one more taste of him, either.

She lowered her hands to press them against his chest. Felt his heart beating fast under her palms.

And knew she mustn't wound that heart any more than she already had.

Beth reluctantly pushed harder against him. Tom withdrew, a questioning look on his face.

"I want to finish my story," she explained. "You deserve to hear the rest."

A brief flattening of his lips was the only sign of his indecision, but it was enough to make Beth's determination waver. Oh, those sexy lips...

"Okay." He reclined against the cushions and pulled her back into his arms. The warmth of his torso burned through their T-shirts, heating her spine. He threaded his fingers through hers and laid them across her abdomen.

"So go ahead and finish." He kissed the crown of her head, and she never felt so safe and secure.

What was wrong with her that she couldn't believe this feeling could last forever?

"Beth?"

Right. One step at a time. Finish the story about college. Then worry about spending the rest of your life without the man you love.

"Um, yeah. There's really not much more to it. I chose music as my minor, breezed through the courses on music theory and music history. I'd lived through a lot of the recent stuff firsthand, and the rest I'd heard plenty of stories about over the years."

She looked down at the hands enfolding hers. So strong. So capable.

"But what I enjoyed the most—and I hadn't expected to—was the actual music instruction. I took voice lessons and a bit of piano, too. But singing was the best. It was a great way to relieve stress."

Sex was a great stress reliever, too, but she kept that thought to herself. Time for that later. Maybe.

"When I entered the MBA program, I missed the relaxation of music classes. So I joined up with a community chorus. It was fun, and because it only met once a week for a couple hours, it didn't take much time away from studying. We performed at local schools, nursing homes. Things like that. Nothing like what you guys do—what you're asking me to do."

"You'll do great." He placed a kiss on her temple, squeezed her in an encouraging hug. "So what happened after you finished school? Did you stay with the chorus?"

Beth shook her head. "No. I stuck with it for a while, but once Eric and I got together, I quit."

"Did you want to quit?"

"No." The word was out before she could stop it. "I mean, I don't think so. It just sort of happened. Eric would make plans, and I'd go along with them."

Tom was silent, and, once again, Beth felt ashamed of her past behavior.

"At the time, I wanted to be with him so badly it didn't matter that my own plans were dismissed. Pretty pathetic, huh?"

Tom maneuvered so they were once again face-to-face. "No. Not pathetic. Wrong. It was wrong on his part to ignore your interests, your hobbies. Your desires." He grasped her shoulders and gave her a gentle shake. "I don't know why the hell you keep trying to take the blame for what this jerk did to you. From everything you've told me, he was a self-serving, domineering prick."

Her lips twisted into a deprecating smirk. "Yeah. That planting of evidence bit certainly doesn't put him in a good light."

He shook her again. Harder. "That's not what I'm talking about and you know it. By cutting you off—from your own friends, interests, whatever—he was setting you up from the get-go. He wanted your entire existence to revolve around him. He wanted to control you."

Beth pushed up and walked away. "But don't you see? I let him!"

She turned back to Tom, still seated. "I let him have control. I lost myself to the point I didn't care that I wasn't singing anymore, or having dinner with girlfriends. I allowed it to be all about him."

Tom extended an arm, inviting her back to the sofa. Wanting his comfort, his nearness, she reclaimed her seat next to him.

He wrapped his arms around her, tucked her head beneath his chin, and kissed her hair. "In a healthy relationship, it should always be about them. Two people are involved. And both of them are risking their hearts, their souls, in order to stay together. If both parties don't support and appreciate the individuality of the other, the relationship won't work."

Beth raised her head. "How did you get so profound? Is this some of your yoga teachings coming through?"

"Nope. No yoga." He shrugged. "It's just that my parents had a great marriage. They were together nearly thirty-five years before my mom died. They had their little quarrels, and there was a lot of compromise, but they were always there for each other. And I want a marriage as strong as theirs was."

Marriage.

How did they get onto that topic?

If he'd meant to get her mind off her affair with Eric, he'd succeeded. But it was best to move on. Literally.

She once again rose to her feet. "Well, I know nothing about good marriages, but I do know about good food. And my stomach wants some real bad."

She walked to the door and looked back. "Ready for lunch?"

He shook his head but still joined her, a smile on his face. He reached past her to open the door. "You just love to keep me guessing, don't you?"

"Right back atcha, buddy."

His smile widened into a grin before he leaned down to kiss her forehead. Then he took her hand and led her down the hall.

"Let's go eat."

•

Something was different in Tom's performance tonight.

He still looked scrumptious. Still sang and played awesomely.

But he had a new vibe about him. An extra bit of energy.

She let her gaze roam all around, searching the concert hall, the audience, the stage, for what was responsible for the change.

Maybe he'd already received the gift she'd arranged for him at the front desk. She'd asked that it be delivered when Tom returned to his room after the concert, but the clerk could have messed up.

And that meant Tom's edginess was due to his impatience to meet with her after the show. Alone, for the first time ever.

She'd spent almost eight months walking past Crowley's Hardware on a daily basis, hoping for a glimpse of him through the store's large windowpanes.

There would be no reason for someone of her social class to enter a hardware store, so why draw attention to herself? Men like Tom preferred a more subtle approach. She was sure of it.

He came from a working-class family, but he deserved high-class treatment all the way. Which was why she'd had delivered an elegant fruit tray consisting of luscious strawberries, grapes, pears, apples, and oranges.

Of course, the warm caramel and chocolate fondues would be useless if her gift was sent too early, but she could quickly have them replaced. And in the meantime there was always the whipped cream...

A dreamy smile crossed her face as she momentarily got lost in her thoughts, and when she refocused on the present, Tom was standing by the back-up singers. Which didn't bother her because Tom often moved around the stage when he wasn't singing.

But as she continued to fixate on him, she noticed he spent an extraordinary amount of time near the blonde in the black dress.

Wait. She was sure there hadn't been a blonde back-up singer in Roadhouse's previous shows.

She fumbled through the tour program she held—her eleventh one—scanning over the photo spreads of the band.

No, the only blondes pictured were Leo and Jack. No blonde

woman anywhere.

She'd thought the backing vocals had sounded a bit off.

The girl's eyes narrowed as she followed Tom's movements, watching as he threw numerous smiles in the blonde's direction.

This had to stop. And it would, after tonight.

Tom would find the note she'd written him, directing him to her room and instructing him to bring her gift along with him.

Erotic visions of feeding each other fresh fruit, drizzling caramel and chocolate over each other's body only to lick it off, took over.

She lost track of what was happening on stage, but it didn't matter. She knew the entire song list by heart, and what happened later, with Tom, was going to be the most exciting event of her night.

Of her life.

Because it was the start of their new life. Together.

Before she knew it, Leo was introducing the band members.

She clapped appropriately for Sam, Jack, and Dylan, but then whistled, screamed, and shouted her head off for Tom. Even though her parents would disapprove of her actions, saying she was making a fool of herself, she didn't care.

She would do anything for Tom.

And then Leo got to the back-up singers. "And last, but certainly not least. Ladies and gentlemen, let me present two very lovely and talented ladies."

She waited.

"Hannah Patterson ..." The redhead smiled and waved to the audience.

"... and Beth Miller!" Now the blonde received her acknowledgement from the crowd.

The girl once again opened the program, this time looking for the band listing. Under "Backing Vocals" were the names Hannah Patterson and Elizabeth Garcia.

So who was this other woman, and where had she come from?

And then her eyes caught the name Bethany Miller. It was listed under the category "Crew Personnel."

A roadie.

The woman was a roadie.

There was only one way that a woman hired to haul equipment could attain the status of singer: She had somehow tricked Tom into helping her.

Obviously Bethany Miller was a money-grubbing tart who was trying to sink her claws into him.

Well, the blonde could still sing if she wanted, but that was all she could have. After tonight, the woman would know her plan to seduce Tom wasn't going to work.

Because Tom loved her. And this Beth was nothing to him.

Nothing.

Chapter Eleven

Tom couldn't stop watching Bethany.

She was clear on the other side of the room, talking and laughing with Hannah, Jack, and Sam, and he couldn't stop looking at her.

Prior to tonight, he would've told the world he thought she was beautiful. But not now.

Because at this moment, she was beyond her usual beauty. She was absolutely stunning.

Her everyday stylings were gone.

No more long braid or ponytail with a baseball cap. No more simple applications of eyeliner and lip-gloss. No more jeans, T-shirt, and sneakers.

With Hannah's help, Beth had transformed into a vivacious siren. And just like the sailors of lore, he was helpless to ignore her call.

Tom's gaze drifted over her. Her face was professionally made up so as not to appear washed out on stage. But now, instead of looking garish under the suite's softer lighting, the cosmetics served only to emphasize her eyes and cheekbones. And her lips were outlined with a plum-red shade to match her eye shadow.

Watching those lips curve around the rim of her wineglass, then seeing her throat work as she swallowed a sip of the alcohol—it made his blood boil.

He shifted his gaze upward as Beth continued to converse with her new friends.

Her long blonde tresses now had soft curls in them, and the sides were held back with rhinestone barrettes. Dangling rhinestone earrings drew attention to her delicate collarbones, exposed by the thin straps of her short black dress.

It should have been funny that Liz and Hannah wearing the

exact same dress had no effect on him, but Tom knew the feelings he had for Bethany made all the difference.

Taking a sip of his draft beer, he continued to follow the lines of Beth's slender body as she moved to speak with another group of people. Firm breasts supported by the dress's fitted bodice, exposing just the right amount of cleavage to entice, but not appear tacky.

A trim waist, flat stomach, and nicely curved hips. Shapely legs that seemed even longer encased in black stockings and two-inch heels.

He couldn't wait to feel those legs wrapped around his waist. But, unfortunately, it wouldn't be tonight.

This little impromptu after-concert party for the band and crew would last a while longer, and since it was taking place in Roadhouse's suite, there was no way Tom could abscond with Beth without appearing obvious.

Besides, the celebration was really in Bethany's honor anyway.

Tonight's show had gone off without a hitch, mostly due to her hard work over the past two days. As promised, the members of Roadhouse had spent most of that time rehearsing, trying to prepare Beth for tonight's performance.

And she had done her part more than adequately. Rehearsing songs, practicing dance moves, going over the stage entrances and exits and other general performance procedures—it was a wonder if any one of them had gotten a sufficient amount of sleep.

But he was wide-awake now, and enough was enough. It was his turn to be with Beth.

They'd been so busy since arriving in Reading that they hadn't had a single moment alone together. Not since that first morning, when Bethany had explained about her singing.

But he was sure that would change when they departed for Erie the next day. The panic of finding a replacement for Liz was over, and the final shows could go smoothly.

As long as Eric Sharpe continued to stay away, that is. And that was one more reason for him to stay close to Beth. To protect her from her ex.

As he took another drink of beer, Tom's eyes moved slowly over Beth again.

Yeah, like he needed another excuse to be near her.

Like loving her wasn't reason enough.

Bethany's gaze suddenly met his, and she froze in place, stopping in mid-sentence with her hands in the air. But then she regained her composure and turned back to Mike and Dylan. She must have excused herself because she headed over toward him, a wide smile on her face.

He pushed off the bar he'd been lounging against and went to meet her halfway. They stopped, toe-to-toe, in the middle of the parlor.

"Hi," she said softly.

"Hi," he replied the same way.

She cast her gaze downward and took a quick sip of her wine.

She was nervous.

Hmm. All evening she'd been laughing and socializing like the belle of the ball that she was. But as soon as she had his undivided attention, she got nervous?

This could be a good sign …

"Want to go out on the balcony for a while? You look like you could use some fresh air."

Okay, that was definitely not true. She looked terrific. But if he could get her semi-alone with that line, then what the hell.

"Sure. That sounds great." She turned to circumvent the buffet tables and head toward the French doors. Tom moved to follow her, but came to a halt as Cole stepped in front of them.

"Hey, Beth! Congrats on your first night as a singer!"

"Thanks, Cole."

Tom tuned out the rest of their conversation. He was sure Beth had heard similar comments from the other partygoers, and the praise was well deserved. But his mind wasn't on what had happened earlier on stage.

It was on what he wanted to happen when they went out on the balcony.

Tom idly looked over the buffet choices laid out on two adjoining tables. Fancy pastries and quiches sat next to mini corn dogs and pizzas. There was something for everyone.

Right in front of him, there was even a tray of fruit for those who didn't want something too heavy at this late hour.

At first Tom had thought the item was a little odd to have at a post-concert shindig, but then he'd forgotten about it. He'd been focused on Bethany.

And now, as she wound down her exchange with Cole, Tom focused on her again.

He popped a couple of grapes into his mouth and sat his half-full glass of beer down on the large fruit tray. He wanted both hands empty when he went outside with Beth.

Tom placed a hand at the small of Bethany's back, and she turned to him with another brilliant smile.

"Ready?" he asked.

She nodded, and they moved toward the open balcony doors once again.

He'd never noticed the pink card emblazoned with his name on it, now hidden beneath his glass.

•

Beth felt the heat of Tom's large hand on her back as he guided her outside, and the adrenaline rush she'd felt while performing came back tenfold.

They'd all worked so hard the last two days that she longed to be alone with him, even if it was just to talk.

Because talking with Tom was more enjoyable, more exciting, than making love with Eric had ever been. And knowing that, she was dying to experience the latter with Tom.

She suspected she'd probably lose her mind from the sensory overload, but she couldn't wait to go mad.

The late night air felt cool on her bare shoulders, pleasant after the crowded warmth of the suite. Beth moved to the balcony's side railing, resting her elbows on its top. The sheer drapes on the French doors, along with artfully placed floral arrangements, guaranteed them almost complete privacy from people inside.

"So how did it feel to sing in front of a packed auditorium?" Tom leaned back against the railing next to her, arms bent behind him so his hands could clasp the upper rail.

The pose drew attention to his powerful arm and chest muscles, straining against his snug gray shirt. Black jeans and boots completed his outfit, emphasizing his lean, sexy build. From all angles, too.

With his attractive backside in her direct view for most of the concert, she'd had a heck of a time trying to stay focused. The man's body was utterly touchable.

So what was stopping her?

Beth stepped in front of Tom and wrapped her arms around his narrow waist. He immediately widened his stance and locked his arms around her, pulling her tight against him.

Her heels put them eye-to-eye with one another, their bodies aligned perfectly from breast to groin.

"You all right?" he asked. "You cold?"

She shook her head. "I'm perfect."

Beth leaned forward to press a gentle kiss against his lower jaw. It was baby smooth beneath her lips, unlike the other morning.

"I just wanted to say thank you. Singing tonight, in front of all those people—it's something I'll never forget."

He smiled. "Now don't be talking like it's a one-time thing. We've still got plenty of shows left. You're not going anywhere."

Maybe not today, or next week. But she'd be leaving soon after that. She had to.

Beth lifted a hand to comb through his dark hair, loving the feel of it between her fingers. His eyes closed and a low groan escaped his lips. "Yes," she said, "but the first time is the most memorable, don't you think? It's a completely new experience. You're doing something you never did before, maybe to conquer old fears or..."

She trailed off as his eyes opened. Heat emanated from them. Desire. For her.

"The first time may seem the most daunting, and the most amazing, but every time after that has it's own rewards. You can make every experience as new and exciting as you want. It's all in what you bring to the moment. What you feel."

Right then she had the feeling he wasn't talking about performing anymore.

And that was fine with her.

She didn't know who moved first, or if it was a mutual thing, but in the next instant their lips were crushed together, hungrily clinging and then opening to taste the very depths of each other.

She moved her arms so she could delve into his hair once again, then brushed her fingers over his ears, cheekbones, jaw. She couldn't stop touching him.

His grip tightened even more, his hands sliding down to knead her bottom and pull her so close she could clearly feel his erection pressing against her abdomen. So close, yet so far from where she wanted— No. *Needed* it to be.

He tore his mouth away, then leaned his forehead against hers. "Ah, sweetheart, you don't know what you do to me."

"I think I could make a good guess," she said in between deep breaths. "If I had one of those things, we'd be having a sword fight right now."

He tilted his head back and laughed. "Oh, man. That's what I love about you. You don't mince words."

Tom pressed tender kisses along her hairline while his strong hands rubbed up and down her back. His caresses felt wonderful, but Beth's mind was in a whirl.

Love? Did he say love?

That's what I love about you.

Wait, she shouldn't get carried away. Those words could be thrown at a person for any number of reasons, usually in a platonic manner. It certainly didn't mean he loved her.

He was just coining a phrase. Wasn't he?

Beth leaned back to look into Tom's face, at his twinkling brown eyes and broad grin. Had she really been hoping, deep down, that Tom would fall in love with her and they'd live happily ever after?

Get a grip, girl. Life on the road sucks and you know it. Even if he did love you, that's not what you want for yourself.

The familiar refrain from Beth's inner voice was right, and she knew it.

But another inner voice suddenly appeared, and it said what she wanted was moot. It was what she needed that mattered.

And she needed Tom.

Desperate to stop the turmoil in her head, wanting only to experience all the present had to offer, Beth gripped Tom's head and ravaged his mouth with every bit of energy she could muster.

He returned the embrace full-force, wrapping her long hair around his fingers in order to hold her still.

But she wasn't going anywhere. This was exactly where she wanted to be.

In his arms. Forever.

Oops. There was that annoying second voice again, sticking its nose into business that had been settled years ago.

Needing even more distraction, Beth forced Tom's arm downward, leading his hand to her breast.

Another low groan came from his lips, and he instantly molded his fingers around her curved flesh, extremely sensitive beneath the dress she wore. The style of the clingy spandex hadn't allowed for a bra, so her taut nipple was clearly outlined through the black material.

Tom pulled his head back to look down at what his ministrations had done to her. "Oh, darlin', you are so beautiful."

He came forward again to kiss her while his hand moved to slide the thin strap of her dress off her shoulder.

Wanting his skilled fingers on her bare skin, Beth didn't utter a single sound of protest. She'd completely forgotten other people were less than six feet away.

"Hannah, we need to talk about this!"

But the memory of where they were came rushing back as Jack and Hannah erupted through the French doors and onto the balcony next to them.

Tom dropped his arms and stepped away, keeping Beth out of view just enough for her to subtly readjust her dress.

"Jack, I told you I'm fine—oh, hi, Tom." Hannah's eyes widened at the sight of Beth next to him. "And Beth?" Avid curiosity was so apparent on the woman's face that Beth decided maybe she hadn't been as subtle as she'd thought.

Jack shot Hannah a quelling look. Then he addressed Tom and Beth, his questioning gaze moving between them. "We're not interrupting anything, are we?"

Tom quirked an eyebrow at his friend. "Maybe I should be asking you the same thing."

Hannah sent Jack an indecipherable glance, but the two of them remained silent.

When a minute had elapsed with no one speaking, Beth decided to break the stalemate. "Tom, we should probably go back inside anyway."

"Yeah, all right." He once again laid a guiding hand on her lower back, and they moved past Hannah and Jack and into the light spilling out of the suite. "See you two later."

"See ya." Beth added her own goodbye to Tom's.

"Hey, Tom," Hannah said, "wait a minute." She dug into the tiny purse hanging off her shoulder and came up with a tissue. She handed it to Tom. "Wipe your mouth."

Beth looked closely at Tom's face as Hannah continued on. "Plum Passion looks better on Beth than it does on you."

Tom grinned as he wiped traces of Beth's lipstick from his face, but Beth felt a flush rise over her own skin.

The man had driven her crazy with lust in public places too many times. And he might be enjoying himself, but she couldn't take it anymore.

The next time they engaged in a make-out session, it would be in private. And she was determined their activities would follow through to their natural, mutually satisfying end.

Three weeks of foreplay was enough, for God's sake.

As Tom and Beth re-entered the parlor, the slim figure on a nearby balcony turned and went back inside her own room, slamming the door shut behind her.

•

The trip to Erie, Pennsylvania, and the ensuing performance there were uneventful—a blessed change from the hubbub surrounding the previous shows.

Throughout the concert and the autograph session afterward, Beth had been riding high due both to the crowd's energy and to Tom Crowley. His proximity to her on stage and at the signing table later on was a big tease: Look but don't touch.

It made her want to scream.

So as they arrived back at their hotel, Beth was torn. On one hand, she wanted to grab Tom and shove him into the first empty room they came across. Broom closet, public rest room, it didn't matter. She just wanted him alone and naked.

But on the other hand, the adrenaline rush that had kept her going before was severely depleted, leaving her fighting to keep her eyes open. She wanted nothing more than a leisurely soak in her room's big tub, but she was afraid she'd end up drowning if she tried it.

"Poker in our suite. You girls up for it?" Leo apparently was still raring to go, even at this late hour.

As the group filed into the elevator, Hannah said, "Yeah, I'm game. How about you, Beth?"

She gave a weak smile in reply. "Sorry, guys. The way I feel right now, I wouldn't be much of a challenge to beat."

"Oh, come on. Compared to how Dylan plays, you'd be giving

us a run for our money!" Jack's comment started a bout of good-natured teasing among Hannah and the guys, with everybody voicing an opinion of the others' poker skills.

They all had such fun together that Beth wished she had the stamina to join their card game. But she was totally wiped out.

Good thing they had time to recoup before their final concerts. Which meant the tour was almost over, and that thought made her head, and heart, ache.

Yeah, a long soak was definitely what she needed in order to forget about things for a while.

The elevator doors opened and everyone stepped out. Hannah moved to the right, saying to the men, "Give me about twenty minutes. I'm gonna shower and change first."

Tom grasped Beth's wrist, pulling her aside as Hannah and the guys went their separate ways down the hall.

"Are you sure you're not up to playing? Or even just hanging out with us?" His eyes searched her face. "Never mind. I can see how tired you are. Maybe we can do something tomorrow?"

She nodded and gave him a weary smile, then pulled his head down to kiss his cheek. "Thank you for understanding."

So much for her drag-Tom-into-a-janitor's-closet-and-jump-his-bones idea. With her luck, she would've fallen asleep in a mop bucket as soon as his clothes were off.

"I'll walk you to your room," he said, taking her hand and leading her down the hall.

Minutes later, Beth was sprawled out, face down and fully dressed, on her double bed.

She knew she wouldn't have made it through a bath, but she couldn't even muster the energy for a quick shower. Perhaps after a short nap she'd feel better...

"Hey, Beth." Someone was shaking her leg. "Hey, sweetie, you should change."

Beth turned her head to find Hannah sitting on the bed next to her, freshly showered and dressed in an olive tank and capris. A white sweater was draped over her shoulders to guard against the hotel's overworked air conditioning.

"Man, you weren't kidding when you said you were tired. I wasn't in the bathroom more than ten minutes and you were dead to the world. But you wouldn't be comfortable sleeping in that dress all night, so I figured I'd better wake you before I left."

Hannah gave a friendly pat to Beth's back and then stood. "It's too bad you don't feel well. When we play poker it usually turns into an all-night thing." She smiled as Beth rolled to her back. "So there I'll be, crashing in the guys' suite, and you'll be in this room all alone. Kind of sucks, doesn't it?"

Beth rolled her eyes. That was the understatement of her life lately. "Gee, thanks for pointing that out."

She stood and stretched her arms over her head. Since she was up, she may as well take that shower. It might refresh her even more than her catnap had. And then maybe she'd see about getting Tom's attention off of cards and onto her...

As Beth kicked off her heels and moved toward the bathroom, Hannah took a last look at herself in the wall mirror. "You sure you don't want to come along?" she asked as she fluffed her bangs. "I can wait."

"No, you go ahead," Beth replied. "I may come by later, but I'm not sure yet."

Hannah smiled once again and let out a muffled chuckle. "Want me to save you some time and effort? I'll just tell Tom to get his ass down here pronto. You won't even need to get dressed. I'll give him my key card and you can wait in the bed for him ... naked!"

Beth joined in with Hannah's laughter even as she grabbed a nearby pillow and tossed it at her friend's head.

The sad thing was, she was seriously considering taking Hannah up on her suggestion.

"Okay, okay. I won't say anything to him." Hannah's expression turned serious. "But I hope you do. You guys deserve some special time together. Everyone can see you really care about each other."

Beth's own smile slipped. "Thanks, Hannah. You're a good friend. I'm glad we met."

"Me, too." The women moved to give each other a quick hug.

"Now," said Hannah, stepping back, "I'm off to whup some guys' butts in poker." She pulled open the door and began to step into the hall. "Ooh! A present!"

Hannah leaned down to pick a festive-looking box off the floor. Beth moved to her side as Hannah looked at the gift tag. "Rats. It's for you." She looked at Beth and arched an eyebrow. "Looks like someone else doesn't want to spend the night alone."

"Oh, stop it," was Beth's reply as she took the package from Hannah. It was a florist's box.

Now, how could Tom arrange for a flower delivery at this time of night? Unless he'd received the box earlier and had waited to put it outside her door.

Maybe Hannah was right, and he, too, had hoped for a different end to this evening.

Well, Beth was fully awake now, so satisfying their mutual desires before the sun rose was a distinct possibility. She smiled as she loosened the huge red bow holding the box together.

Wouldn't it be fun to tease Tom with his gift? To lightly drag the flowers over his body, barely grazing his skin with the velvet-soft petals, tickling him in his most sensitive areas?

She couldn't wait.

But as she lifted the lid off the package, Beth's smile froze, and she did something that was totally out of character.

She screamed.

Chapter Twelve

At the sound of Beth's scream echoing in the hallway, Tom dropped the beer bottles he'd been carrying and raced toward her room.

What he saw stunned him.

Beth stood in the open doorway of the room, eyes wide and hands clasped over her mouth. At her feet was an open box. Black roses, complete with thorn-laden stems, spilled out onto the gray carpet.

The flowers were covered by black and white flecks which, on closer inspection, turned out not to be the floral potpourri he'd thought. They were animated masses of maggots, beetles, and spiders.

And while Beth stood petrified, a look of horror on her face, Hannah angrily stomped on any creature that dared to venture too far from the box, cursing all the while.

Hannah threw Tom an indignant glance as he knelt to gather as much of the mess as possible back into the package. "Can you believe someone would do this to her? How disgusting—gotcha!" She slammed her sandaled foot down onto a spider making its way toward Beth's stocking-clad toes.

"Not just anyone. Eric Sharpe." After securing the box's lid, Tom stood and dusted off his hands. "Why don't you get Beth inside? We need to call security." He took another look at Beth's face. "And possibly a doctor."

Upon entering the room, Hannah ushered Bethany into the bathroom while Tom headed toward the phone. "Why don't you get out of those clothes and take a long, hot shower?" Hannah suggested. "We can take care of everything out here, sweetie. You just try to relax."

Tom couldn't make out Beth's muffled response, but he heard

the water come on soon after. As he completed his call to hotel security, Hannah came out of the bathroom and shut the door behind her. She handed Tom a soapy washcloth and dry hand towel.

"Here. Get that nasty grime off your hands. Ick!"

Tom raised an eyebrow at her as he followed her instructions. "I wouldn't have thought you'd be afraid of a few bugs."

"Afraid of bugs? No. I can handle the creepy-crawlies." Hannah took the dirty linens from Tom and threw them on a bureau. "It's the sentiment behind the gift that scares the crap out of me. The flower of death, along with oodles of squirming critters? Not good."

To say the least, Tom thought. He glanced at the closed bathroom door. "Are you sure we should be leaving her alone in there? I don't want her to pass out and get hurt."

The thought of Beth crashing through the glass shower doors made his stomach turn, just as it had when he'd heard her scream.

"She'll be fine. There's a bench in the stall she can sit on if she feels faint. But I'll check on her anyway, if you want."

"Yeah, I want." Tom glanced at the bedside clock and started for the door. "Security should be here by now. And they're bringing the local PD, too."

He grabbed the door handle but then turned back to Hannah. "I'll fill them in about Beth's history with Sharpe, but they'll probably need to ask you questions about the package. I'll leave the door cracked open in case we have to get you."

He headed out as Hannah asked, "What about Beth?"

"She doesn't need any more aggravation tonight. I'll tell the cops she'll contact them tomorrow." He stepped into the hall in time to see four men coming toward him, two in suits and two in security uniforms.

Forty-five minutes later, the quartet left with all the information Tom and Hannah could provide about the package's possible origin. And while the detectives bagged the florist's box as evidence, the security guards were instructed to monitor all activities on the floor, especially arrivals via the stairs and elevators.

Tom was happy to see the men depart. The message discovered among the flowers had made him especially eager to get back to Bethany's side. To see that she was safe. And to hold her.

As he and Hannah re-entered the room, his eyes sought Beth out. Enveloped in a plush hotel robe and scrubbed free of all cosmetics, she was sitting Indian-style in the middle of the closest double bed, hands wrapped around a steaming Styrofoam cup.

Hopefully there was something decaffeinated in the container so that she could get some sleep.

"What's going on? Are they gone?" Beth's gaze bounced between Tom and Hannah and finally settled on Tom as he moved to sit on the bed next to her.

He'd never thought the first time they occupied the same bed would be under circumstances like this.

"Things are taken care of for the night, but tomorrow the three of us need to go to the police station to be fingerprinted. They need to separate our prints from any others the crime lab finds on the box."

"Do you think they'll find any at all? Besides ours, I mean?"

"There's a better chance of finding them on the box than anywhere else. The elevator lobby and stairwells would have too many prints to count because they're high traffic areas."

Tom glanced at Hannah. "And Hannah explained to the detectives that the package was just sitting on the floor outside the room, so it's doubtful the sender even touched the door to leave prints. The package, and what was inside it, is the most they have to go on at this point."

Beth's eyes narrowed. "What do you mean, 'what was inside it?' They can trace the origin of the flowers? And the insects?"

"I'm sure they'll look into that stuff, too, the best they can." He hesitated. "But there was something else in there. I must have pushed it under the box when I cleaned up."

"Okay, what was it?" When he didn't immediately respond, Beth expelled a harsh breath. "Tom, I'm not a baby! Just tell me already!"

Needing to touch her, to soothe her in any way possible, Tom reached out to take Beth's hand. She may not need comfort right now, but he certainly did.

"There was a note inside the box. It was typewritten, so it'll be more difficult to analyze than a handwritten one. But I'm sure they'll figure it out."

"Tom, you're stalling." Beth's aggravation was evident both in her voice and in the firm squeeze she gave his hand. "Just tell me what the note said."

The message on the plain white card was indelibly etched into his memory. "It said, 'You have ruined all my plans and caused me a lot of pain. I look forward to returning the favor.'"

As Tom spoke, he watched the color drain from Bethany's face. If she hadn't taken Eric Sharpe's threat seriously before, she did now.

The phone rang, startling the three occupants of the room. Hannah moved to answer it while Tom continued to rub Beth's hand. He wished he could make all of this go away, but he couldn't. All he could do was be there for Beth however she needed him to be.

"That was Dylan," Hannah said as she hung up the phone. "The guys wanted to know what was taking me so long." She headed for the door. "I'm going to let them know what happened. The more people who can keep an eye out for this creep, the better."

As Hannah reached for the handle, Beth spoke up. "Don't tell my father! Or any of the techs. Please?"

"But ..." Hannah left her question unasked as Beth turned away to focus her pleading gaze on Tom.

"I won't have a moment's peace if he hears about this. He won't want me out of his sight!"

Ah, now he understood. In spite of the danger she was obviously in, Beth still wanted to spend time alone with him. To pursue a relationship with him. The part of his mind that wanted to protect Bethany at all costs was quickly overridden by his lustful cravings to make love with her.

Breaking eye contact with Beth, he turned to Hannah and said, "Let the fellows know that Beth wants to keep this quiet, okay?"

Hannah looked at the two of them sitting on the bed, and she remained silent for a long moment. Then the redhead gave a decisive-looking nod. "Sure. I'll do that." She pulled the door open, looked down at the freshly cleaned area at her feet, and took a wide step over it. "Catch you two later," she added before the door clicked shut behind her.

•

As soon as Hannah left, Beth stretched to put her cup of coffee on the night stand. Then she uncrossed her legs and slid off the side of the bed farthest from Tom. She walked to the window and pulled the drapes back, pretending an interest in the city's skyline.

In reality, she wanted nothing more than to be in Tom's arms. Not just because she wanted comfort—damn Eric, anyway!—but because she yearned to experience his loving.

But as she'd told herself before, there would be no more fooling around with Tom unless they could finish it. And since there was no telling when Hannah would return, it was best to keep her distance from the man, no matter how hard it was.

"So what were you doing coming back here? I thought you were going to play poker with everyone else." Beth watched Tom's reflection in the window as he rose from the bed and headed toward her.

Despite her determination to avoid physical contact with him, her heart beat heavily in her chest and her breathing quickened. The anticipation of his touch and in fact, his very nearness, did that to her. It was inevitable.

Beth let the curtain drop back into place as she turned around. Tom stood not six inches away, his eyes showing a mixture of emotions. Concern was there, but desire was even more overwhelmingly evident in his molten gaze.

"I didn't want to be with everyone else," he said. "I wanted to be with you." With that, he leaned down to brush her lips with his own.

Against her better judgment, Beth wrapped her arms around his neck, pressed her mouth more firmly against his. A soft moan rose from her throat, but the sound was absorbed into Tom's mouth as he hungrily returned her kiss.

Lost in his embrace, the ringing of the hotel phone barely penetrated Beth's foggy mind. But Tom heard it, and he stepped back to grab the receiver.

"Yeah? Oh, hi." A long pause. "All right, thanks. Thanks a lot." Then he hung up and looked at Beth, still standing by the window. "That was Hannah. She's going to stay with the guys for the rest of the night."

His statement dissolved any remaining reservations Beth had harbored. They had the whole night—or what was left of it, anyway, since it was nearing one AM—to be together. They could make love at last.

So why was Tom walking to the door? Had she been so wrong in thinking he wanted her, too?

Beth watched as he turned the deadbolt and slid the security chain into place. He turned to face her, yet still remained near the door.

"I want you so much." His words caused shivers of excitement to course through her body. "But after what happened, I need to be sure you really want—"

Beth untied her robe and pushed it off her shoulders.

"—to do this," he finished unsteadily.

She stood naked before him. If he couldn't interpret that as a firm yes, then she didn't know what else she could do to convince him.

Tom took long strides across the room, pulling his shirt over his head and kicking off his sneakers as he moved. Good. Evidently her message had been clear.

When he stopped in front of her, Beth skimmed her hands across his wide shoulders and firm chest. She trailed her fingers over his small nipples and watched as they grew rigid. She felt the wiry patch of dark hair in the middle of his chest, then moved lower to touch the softer line of hair beneath his navel, visible above his low-slung jeans.

As she reached to unfasten his pants, Tom groaned. "Oh, Bethany," he murmured. "Sweetheart."

She looked deep into his eyes, her hands still busy below. "Touch me," she whispered. "I need you to touch me, too."

Her words seemed to break the invisible restraints that had kept him frozen in place. Tom crushed her into his arms, one hand twisting into her still-damp hair while the other ran rampant over her back and bottom. His lips ravaged hers, nipping, then licking, and finally opening to explore the recesses of her mouth.

She loved it all. Every touch, every groan, every whisper. Finally she would enjoy everything he had to give.

He swung her up into his arms only to move the short distance to the bed and carefully lay her upon it. For a few moments he stood quietly looking down at her, causing thoughts to rush into Beth's head of how similar this was to her dream.

But then Tom quickly pushed down his briefs and unfastened jeans, shedding both them and his socks in mere seconds. His erection sprang proudly upward, and her mind instantly centered on the here and now.

She raised her arms, wanting to feel him next to her. On top of her. Inside her.

Tom immediately responded to her request, moving over her to kneel between her wantonly-spread legs. Beth wrapped her arms around him, stroking his shoulders, back, buttocks. She didn't care how eager she appeared. She wanted him. Now.

But Tom apparently wasn't in as big a rush as she was. Although he began to slide his erect penis up and down against her slick, swollen folds, he made no move to enter her. Instead, he planted his hands beside her head and kissed her as if their lips were the center of the universe. As if the twining of their tongues was the ultimate culmination of their lovemaking.

His tenderness almost made her break down in tears.

But this wasn't a time for crying. It was a time to celebrate. Because now she knew what had been missing in her sexual encounters with Eric: heat.

Tom made her burn as he slowly traced the dips and curves of her body with his hands and mouth. Eric had all of the right moves, the right technique to get the job done, but it had never made her feel like this.

Now, as Tom leaned down to explore her breast with his tongue, tenderly caressing her hip with his fingertips, she knew why. Eric had been a cold man. And that coldness, that heartlessness, must have permeated through his skills as a lover. Because she knew that Eric had never, ever, made her feel like she was a simmering volcano on the verge of eruption.

Yet Tom had done that from the very first time she'd laid eyes on him. He made her feel alive. Beautiful. And happy.

Even at the best time of their relationship, Eric had simply made her feel comfortable. But she wasn't comfortable now.

Nope, right now she was wound so tight she was about to jump out of her skin. And it felt good.

Beth shoved all thoughts of the past out of her head and concentrated on that good feeling. And it became even more intense as Tom moved his mouth to her other breast, at the same time sliding his hand down to the curls covering her mound.

As he slid a long finger into her feminine core, he leaned up to press another passionate kiss upon her waiting lips. "You are so hot," he murmured just before their lips met.

Tom's fingers continued their fantastic dance in and around her moist sheath. His thumb alternately pressed hard against her clitoris, then circled around it, sending spasms of pleasure through her entire body.

Once again his mouth captured her moan of ecstasy. Needing to catch her breath, she tore her mouth away, panting. Pressure built to an unbearable level inside her, and Beth turned her head to the side, latching on to the muscular forearm beside her like a lamprey in order to suppress the keening wail that longed to escape her throat.

The man's fingers were more talented than she'd ever imagined. And his lips …

Those fine instruments of sensuous torture were busy spreading soft kisses over the exposed area below her ear. As he made his way from her neck to her collarbone, Beth loosened her lip-lock on his arm.

"Tom," she whispered. "I need you. Inside me."

He wriggled his fingers, causing her hips to jerk upward and another groan to slip out. "I am inside you, honey."

He gave one more stroke of his fingers to illustrate his point, and another sound, like that of a cat in heat, came from her mouth.

She slapped him hard on the shoulder. "Don't be a jackass. You know exactly what I mean."

Tom withdrew his fingers from between her thighs and moved back above her, sliding his hair-roughened skin against her on his way up. He captured her face between his palms, and she could smell her sex on his flesh.

He held her gaze as his hips ground against hers, once more teasing her with the possibility of fulfillment. "Yeah. I know. But I want to hear you say it." He leaned down to kiss her cheek. "What do you want, Beth? Tell me."

Beth opened her mouth to speak, but she couldn't do it. No matter how forward she'd been in stripping for him, she couldn't say the words. They remained lodged in her throat.

Well, actions speak louder than words anyway, she thought. So she slid a hand between their bodies and grabbed hold of his erection. She firmly squeezed it and gave a slight upward twisting motion. "This," she said. "Inside me. Now."

A slow smile spread across his face, proving her short but to the point response was quite acceptable.

Tom shifted to the side and leaned over the edge of the bed. She heard him fumble with his discarded jeans and then he repositioned himself to sit back on his heels. In his hands was a condom.

Beth watched as he donned the protection, shocked that she hadn't given it a thought. He looked up and saw her stunned expression. "I don't always carry these around. I was just hoping..."

"It's all right," she said as he trailed off. "It's fine. I'm glad you thought of it."

Tom moved over her again, took her hands into his and intertwined their fingers. He pressed his chest against hers as he pushed her arms back and into the mattress.

"Good," he said softly, his lips closing in on hers. "I'm glad we're in agreement. Because I don't think I could stop at this point."

"Thank God for that," she said, stretching up to seal her lips to his. Tom's tongue thrust into her mouth at the same time his shaft thrust into her wetness. They both groaned at the utter pleasure of him completely filling her.

He rested his forehead against hers. "Oh, baby. You feel so good."

"So do you." She let out a deep breath. "Oh, yeah, so do you."

Tom kissed her forehead, then her lips, clenching her fingers tightly within his own as he slowly began to move his hips. In and out. In and out.

With each thrust, the sensations flowing through Beth grew stronger. Not only between her legs but also in her heart.

As he moved ever faster, she fell deeper and deeper in love with the man. She wrapped her legs around his and pushed her hips upward, eagerly meeting his hot skin with her own.

Tom murmured his approval and rocked even faster, harder. They continued to kiss as their bodies moved together in a rhythm as old as time, until finally he emitted a long groan and shuttered in a release so powerful, and a thrust so deep, that it triggered her own climax.

For the next few minutes, only their erratic breathing and the humming of the air conditioner broke the quiet of the room. Tom released her hands and rolled to his side, pulling her to face him.

He gently trailed his fingers over her cheek, and her eyes lazily drifted closed, a contented smile on her face. "Any regrets?" he asked.

"Yeah." When his fingers stopped moving, Beth forced her lids to open once again. "That we didn't do this sooner."

Tom rolled his eyes, then gave her a hasty kiss. "Lord almighty, darlin'. You almost gave me a heart attack." He slid to the edge of the bed and got up. As he walked toward the bathroom, he threw back assuredly, "Don't worry. We'll definitely be making up for lost time."

The door swung closed behind him, and Beth rolled to her back, her smile growing bigger. She stretched her satisfied body, grateful that reality had far surpassed her imagination.

Tom emerged from the bathroom and came back to sit by her side. "What's that smile for? You happy or something?" His gorgeous mouth curved upward into a grin that matched hers.

"Or something," she answered pertly.

He combed his fingers through her hair, pulling a section of it forward to lie across her breast. The cool, damp strands made her nipple pucker, and the ever-present longing she felt for Tom surged higher once more. He continued to watch her, his hand resting just below the swell of her bosom.

And, slowly, the smile faded from his face. "Are you sure you're doing okay? I want you to tell me if you need anything. That little gift you got earlier had to have shocked you, at the least. And I want you to know that I'm here for you."

Beth reached up to cradle his firm jaw. "Thank you. But I'm fine now. You've already seen to my immediate relaxation, and I'm sure security will take care of the rest. I don't want what's happened to ruin the rest of the tour."

Furrows appeared as his dark brows pulled together, and he shook his head. "I don't understand how you can act so calm. I know this has been weighing on your mind—the possibility that Eric Sharpe is pursuing you."

She felt a bit strange having this conversation with Tom when they were both naked, but evidently it couldn't be avoided. "What makes you think that? I've told you over and over since Baltimore that I doubt Eric would waste his time coming after me."

"That's just it. You've said and done things to fool others—maybe even yourself—but all your fears about Sharpe came out anyway."

"Huh?" She waved her hands in the air, exasperated. "I have no idea what you're talking about."

"Your dream." Tom stood up and paced to the window. He turned to face her, one hand on his hip and the other buried in his short, dark hair. "The one you had on the bus. I know it wasn't about your mother."

Oh, damn. "Tom—"

"It was about Sharpe." He resumed pacing back and forth between the bed and window. "You were terrified about him coming to get you, to hurt you, so you made up that load of crap when Cole mentioned the dream at breakfast."

"Tom, actually—"

"And I just can't stand the fact that you won't admit to anyone—especially me—that you're scared!"

"Tom, listen to me!"

That finally got his attention. He stood still, silent and waiting.

Beth should've known she'd have to come clean about this. It seemed like nothing escaped his notice lately.

She sighed and pushed up to lean against the wooden headboard. "Sit down. I have to be honest with you about something."

He immediately sat next to her hip and picked up her hand. "Anything. You can tell me anything." He pressed a soft kiss into her palm.

She chewed her lower lip for a moment, pondering her best course of action. In the end she decided to just get it over with. "I wasn't dreaming about Eric on the bus. I was dreaming about you."

The look on Tom's face would've been comical if the topic under discussion weren't so serious.

"Say what?"

She exhaled loudly once more, embarrassed to have to explain her thoughts. Beth focused on a point over Tom's shoulder and rushed to get it all out. "I was having a sexual fantasy about you, but I couldn't very well explain that to everybody, so I made up that lame story about my mother's accident and the motion of the bus."

She forced herself to meet his incredulous gaze. "It had nothing to do with Eric. Honestly."

His lips twisted sideways for a quick second, and Beth couldn't tell if it'd been the start of a smile or a frown. Regardless, he instantly schooled his handsome features into an unreadable expression.

"So you expect me to believe you'd been dreaming about me, huh?"

Beth cocked an eyebrow at him. "Yes, I do. It really is the truth, you know."

"Prove it."

Now she was the one to ask, "Say what?"

"Prove to me that you'd been having a sexual fantasy about the two of us. What did we do?"

She couldn't believe he was making her do this. "Umm, well I was lying on the bed naked and you were standing next to me."

He stood up. "Like this?"

"Yeah, except you still had jeans on."

Tom glanced down at his lower half before recapturing her gaze. "We're past that. What's next?"

She spoke softer. "You looked at me, then gave me a massage and kissed me."

His eyes wandered over her body, lingering on spots guaranteed to respond to his attention. His arousal grew more and more noticeable as she watched him watching her.

"I'm not much of a masseuse, so why don't you just tell me where I kissed you." His voice was nearly unrecognizable, it was so thick with desire.

"All over," she whispered, falling further under his spell.

"Hmm," was his response. "I don't think that helps. I need more specific information. Somewhere to start."

"You sucked my toes." Beth clapped a hand over her mouth, but the detail had already slipped past her lips.

"Interesting." Tom moved to the foot of the bed and took hold of her ankles.

"Tom, no—oh!" He pulled her down so quickly she banged her head on the headboard. "Ow!" She rubbed the back of her skull.

"Sorry." That funny sideways twitch flashed across his face again. He trapped her left leg between his thighs then lifted her right leg high, keeping a firm grip on it although she tried her best to pull it away.

"Now, Bethany, how am I supposed to pleasure you if you don't cooperate?"

She couldn't believe he was actually going to do this. Please God, don't let there be carpet lint between her toes.

And she couldn't imagine the view he must be getting with her legs spread open like a Thanksgiving turkey.

"Tom, I don't think..." She trailed off as his tongue darted out to lick the tip of her big toe.

One of his hands kept a grip on her calf while the other slid up from her ankle to grasp her foot, his thumb pressing firmly into the arch.

And she flipped out, crying, "Oh, my God, stop! That tickles!"

The more she flailed around, trying to get her foot free, the more his fingers brushed over her sensitive sole. Ultimately he must have decided it was better to release her than to get kicked in the head.

Beth lay on the mattress trying to catch her breath. And staring disbelievingly at Tom, who was doubled over, holding his stomach because he was laughing so hard.

"What, may I ask, is so funny?"

He took a couple of deep breaths and stood up straight before answering. "You, sweetheart."

"You're laughing at me?"

That sobered him up quick. "Oh, no darlin'."

But Beth caught on rather quick herself. "You were never going to do it, were you? You were just leading me on. Teasing me."

Tom knelt on the bed next to her. "No, I wasn't going to do it, and yes, I was teasing you. But I'd hoped it would lead to fun for both of us." His finger traced a random pattern on her thigh. "And I'd also hoped to move my mouth to a more, shall we say, middle of the road location."

Just like that, her irritation melted away and desire filled her. Again.

"I didn't mean to tickle you—that was an honest mistake. But I really do love to tease you, sweetheart." Tom's hand stopped moving as his burning gaze locked with hers. "And I just really love you."

Chapter Thirteen

Tom hadn't meant for it to come out that way, but he was glad his feelings were out in the open. Settling back on his heels, he waited with bated breath for Beth's response.

Thankfully he didn't have to wait long.

Her beautiful, silver-blue eyes welled up and a tremulous smile formed on her face. "I love you, too, Tom."

He squeezed his eyes shut and let out a deep sigh of relief, for he knew then that everything would be all right. The lurking specter of Eric Sharpe, Beth's dislike of his musician lifestyle—there was nothing they couldn't overcome together.

He stretched out beside Bethany, leaned over to caress her smooth cheek and kiss her still shaky lips. "I love you so much," he said, brushing his lips against her chin, cheek, nose. His hand cupped her breast, fondling its tip until it grew taut. Then he slid down to take her hardened nipple into his mouth.

Over and around, his tongue flicked out to randomly sample her delicious berry-scented flesh. He reveled in the feel of her hands pressing against his head, urging him to taste her more fully.

After giving equal attention to her other breast, Tom shifted to lay between Beth's thighs. He bent her knees and slid his hands beneath her shapely bottom. Her hands drifted over his ears and hair as he kissed his way down her torso.

He paused to dart his tongue in and around her belly button, causing her stomach muscles to clench.

"Tom," she moaned.

"Shh." His goal was within reach, and he would not be deterred from it.

He pushed up on her rear end, at the same time nuzzling through her dark blonde curls to find the sensitive nub hidden within. He gently clamped onto it with his teeth, then circled around it with his tongue, causing a high-pitched cry to emerge from Bethany's throat.

It immediately became his favorite sound, and he was determined to hear it over and over again.

Using every bit of sexual knowledge he possessed, Tom set out to bring Beth to the most powerful climax of her life. Tongue, teeth, lips, hands, his very breath—all were used to pleasure her the best he knew how.

He touched every inch of her womanly center, paying close attention to which areas, and which maneuvers, made her squirm the most.

In the end she made little sound at all.

As he brought her to a shuttering release, tasting her moisture as it flowed over his tongue, she just emitted a long, soft sigh. Her arms fell to the sides, and her chest heaved with each deep breath.

Pleased with his results, Tom placed light kisses on Beth's inner thighs as her body slowly regained equilibrium. Then she leaned up on her elbows, causing her nipples to point at him like two mauve missiles.

"Is that all you got?" she asked with a teasing smile.

He had to laugh. God, he loved her sense of humor.

His arousal was back full strength, and he made sure she could feel it as he eased back up the rumpled bedspread to lie against her.

"Oh, darlin', I've got plenty more to give you." He wrapped his fingers in Bethany's tangled hair and kissed her, allowing her to taste her own juices. She ran her hands over his shoulders, holding him close.

Although he wanted to immediately plunge into her warm, wet depths, he pulled back from her embrace and grabbed another condom from his pants pocket. Beth sat up, too, continuing to touch his upper body as he covered himself. When he finished, he found himself flat on his back with Bethany sitting astride his hips.

She leaned down to kiss his jaw, then whispered, "I think it's time for me to give you something."

And she did just that.

Something exhilarating. Something amazing. Something which

totally turned him inside out.

After lavishing his face and chest with soft kisses, her long hair brushing over his sensitive skin, she reached between them. Lifting her hips, Beth proceeded to slide onto his shaft so slowly, so sweetly, that he couldn't help but thrust his own body upward.

"No," she said. "Let me."

He lowered his pelvis, and she grabbed his hands and placed them on her breasts. Suitably preoccupied, Tom skimmed his fingers over her soft curves as she rode him, her own hands alternately stroking and clutching his chest and stomach.

As her rocking motion drove him nearer to the edge, he ran his hands over her hips and up her back. He drew her down until they lay flush against each other.

"Love you," he murmured once more. Then he hungrily captured her mouth, conveying his feelings in a way that couldn't be confused. At the same time he thrust upward, driving deep into her. Beth's moan vibrated through his mouth, and he thrust again.

He pushed her upright and guided her hips up and down. Her moist sheath welcomed him again and again, and she dug her short fingernails into his skin as they moved together, faster and faster.

At last she flung her head backward and let loose with her now familiar moan of pleasure. When he saw her in the throes of release, her wetness clasping hard around him, he let go, too, and experienced his second life-altering climax of the night.

Beth collapsed on top of him, stretching out her long legs as she tucked her head under his chin. Tom wrapped his arms tight around her and kissed the golden crown of her head. He would've liked to stay in that position all night, but he was still inside her and couldn't risk a leaking condom.

Not to mention the fact that Beth would be an icicle by morning if the air conditioner continued to crank out its Arctic waves directly toward her. And despite her warm body on top of him, Tom was starting to feel somewhat chilled himself.

"Sweetheart," he said, giving Beth's shoulders a little shake. "We have to move."

She took her time sitting up, turning to brush a leisurely kiss across his lips before doing so. Her impish smile and bedroom eyes almost tempted him to have her once more, but Tom resisted the urge.

They both needed rest, and there was still one other thing to do tonight.

So he shifted Bethany onto the mattress and went into the bathroom to clean up. It might seem spontaneous to some, but Tom was sure of what he wanted: Beth at his side for the rest of his life.

However, as he returned to the main room, he realized his question would have to wait until the next day. In the short time he'd left her, Beth had crawled under the brown and green striped bedspread. The steady rise and fall of her back indicated she'd already succumbed to deep sleep.

After dousing the overhead light, Tom made his way to her side and slid in next to her. He pressed a soft kiss to her shoulder and draped an arm around her waist.

His last thought before sleep overcame him was that, despite its horrific beginning, tonight had been the best night of his life.

◆

Last night she'd made the biggest mistake of her life.

That was the first thing to cross Beth's mind when she woke to find Tom's arm wrapped tight around her and his head resting on her back.

She didn't regret what they'd done—she'd never enjoyed herself more—but she was afraid uncomplicated sex was now permanently out of the question.

He'd said he loved her, and she had said the same to him.

So how was this going to affect their parting next week?

It won't, stupid. Guys use the L-word all the time when they're about to get some. It's standard terminology for pre-sex schmoozing. It doesn't mean anything.

Her inner voice was right yet again, but she was sick of listening to the damn thing. Couldn't she just live in the moment for once? Enjoy her time with Tom and escape into the fantasy of happily ever after?

Carefully she rolled to her back, wanting to look at him. He stirred a little as she repositioned herself but otherwise remained unaware of her observations.

His dark hair contrasted sharply with the paleness of her breasts, and she couldn't resist running her fingers through the soft strands. Riding low on his waist, the standard-issue white sheet stood out against the tanned width of his back. She could just see the top edge of his firm butt peeking out from under the cloth, tempting her to pinch it. Gently, of course.

But then again, she could always kiss it better if it hurt too much...

Her hand moved slowly down his broad shoulders and back.

"I need to turn over if you're going to keep heading in that direction." Tom lifted his head and gave her a sexy smile. "We'll both enjoy it a lot more."

She froze.

Oh, yeah, she was in deep trouble. His southern drawl sounded even more attractive with its morning raspiness, but his eyes were what really held her in place. Even in the limited sunlight creeping in between the curtain edges, she could see they were sharp and aware, watching her.

What exactly Tom expected to see, she didn't know.

But Beth did her best to hide her conflicting emotions, plastering a come-hither smile on her face and pushing the sheet away to bare his cheek. She gave it a gentle tap.

"What makes you so sure I wasn't going to have fun?" she asked with a raised eyebrow. "Spanking can be a turn-on if it's done the right way."

Tom shook his head and pushed up. "You expect me to believe you're into that sort of thing?" He stood, unashamed of his nakedness. "Try again."

Beth stayed where she was. "How do you know what I like? You don't really know me. I could have a secret fetish."

"True, but if spanking is it, I'll eat my guitar." He reached down to grab her hand, pulling her off the bed to stand next to him. He cupped her face and stared deep into her eyes. "And I do know you. Don't ever doubt that."

He waited a moment to let his words sink in, then circled around the bed, towing her behind him as he headed toward the bathroom. "Now, for some real fun, let me tell you about a dream I had..."

•

The day passed in a mix of fun and frustration for the two of them.

They shared a shower in the morning, lingering in the spray

until it ran cold. Tom sat on the shower seat and described his dream of her. Beth didn't know when she'd lost her inhibitions with the man, but she wasn't the slightest bit uncomfortable bathing in front of him, following his narrative as she cleansed her body. The whole experience excited her as much as it did him.

The only time she got embarrassed was when she spotted the marks she'd made on Tom's arm and chest the night before.

Tom only laughed at her reaction. "Just goes to show how wild I made you. It means I'm good, sweetheart."

So, of course, after that remark, Beth had to show him how good she was, and how wild she could make him. Giving a wicked smile, she knelt down and proceeded to lavish upon him the sort of personal attention she'd enjoyed the night before.

They both ended up extremely grateful for the presence of that shower bench.

Eventually they emerged from the bathroom sexually satisfied and suitably clean. Beth donned a coral colored sundress before accompanying Tom to his suite so he could change into a fresh white T-shirt and denim shorts. There was no way he was leaving her alone for a second, he told her.

Sitting through the morning meal with various members of the tour entourage was something of a trial. The knowing glances from Roadhouse's members curbed Beth's appetite to the point that her father commented on it. Not wanting to reveal any of the prior night's activities to George, she downed some juice and an English muffin, successfully diverting his attention elsewhere.

Near the closing of the continental breakfast, Tom suggested a local sightseeing excursion. As previously arranged, Hannah asked to come along with the two of them.

Jack's spontaneous decision to join the threesome only added to the plan, in Beth's opinion. However, seeing the sharp look Hannah shot Jack as they left the table, Beth almost regretted his coming with them. Just what was going on between those two, anyway?

Instead of heading directly to the police station to take care of necessary business, Tom insisted upon actually partaking in the tourist attractions he'd mentioned.

The five hours they spent at the planetarium and local historical sites, along with eating junk food from a street vendor, proved very relaxing indeed. And after what transpired with the local law officials, Beth was especially glad they'd been able to enjoy themselves earlier in the day.

She gave her statement regarding the package and her history with Eric. Meanwhile, Tom and Hannah read over their statements from the previous night, verifying their authenticity. The detectives called both the San Francisco and Baltimore police departments to see if there were any leads on Eric's whereabouts, but there was no news.

Beth, Tom, and Hannah were all fingerprinted, but Beth got the feeling the police were just humoring them by that point. There had been no sightings of Eric on the East Coast, and more than likely there would be no evidence recovered that would link him to Beth's little gift.

The group that left the police station was a lot more subdued than the one that had entered. Although they'd been assured all officers in the area were aware of Eric's possible presence, an APB couldn't be issued until officials were sure he was in town. And that he had made contact with Beth.

This stipulation upset Tom to no end.

"I can't believe they won't do anything. He has to attack you before they'll arrest him?" He thrust his hands through his hair, pacing back and forth on the sidewalk as they waited for a taxi.

"Tom, that's not what they said." Beth reached out a hand to stop his rampant movements. "They just have to be sure it's him, and that he really means to harm me."

"Who else would it be?" He spread his arms wide and shrugged his shoulders. "How many other people have threatened to get you for destroying their lives? Huh?"

"Tom—"

"Listen, buster," Hannah interrupted, hands on hips. "We're all worried about Beth—especially those of us who know what happened last night." Her look of disappointment indicated she still wasn't happy that Beth hadn't told her father about the package. "But that's no reason to jump down her throat. It's not going to help the situation."

Tom looked properly chastised. "You're right." He pulled Beth toward him, wrapped his arms around her waist, and pressed a kiss to her forehead. "I'm sorry, sweetheart."

Beth gave a small smile, still a little uncomfortable with his familiarity in front of the others. "It's all right."

"Okay, folks, hold the smooching 'til later." Jack stepped to the curb and lifted an arm. "Cab's here."

"Thank God," Hannah said, pushing past to enter the car first. "My feet are killing me."

Once they were heading back to the hotel, Tom suggested grabbing an early dinner. "Pretzels and hot dogs are great for snacks, but they don't make a meal," he said.

Beth nodded in agreement, but Hannah groaned. "No way. I'm just going to take a long soak and order room service. I think I have blisters on my blisters."

"I'm starved. I'll go with you guys—oomph!" Jack rubbed his ribs and frowned down at Hannah, sitting to his left. "What'd ya do that for?"

She gave him a "you're a complete idiot" look before shaking her head and leaning around him to look at Beth. "Jack won't be joining you two. Sorry." She turned her gaze to Tom in the front seat. "You'll have to make do on your own."

Jack grumbled but otherwise kept silent for the remainder of their short ride.

As soon as the cab stopped, Hannah got out with Jack right on her heels. Beth waited as Tom paid the fare, but she could still hear the others' conversation.

"You are a total numbskull!" Hannah hissed.

"Why, because I'm hungry?"

"No! Because you can't understand the concept of a third wheel!"

"What, like on a tricycle?"

Tom and Beth followed the other couple as they moved toward the hotel entrance. Automatic sliding doors opened to let them pass into the air-conditioned foyer.

"Arrgh!" Hannah threw her hands in the air. "They want to be alone, you idiot! Like, on a bicycle built for two? Is that easy enough for you to understand?"

Tom stopped Beth with a hand on her shoulder, leaving Jack and Hannah continuing on to the elevators alone.

"Ohh ... I like bicycles."

"Yeah, well I prefer unicycles myself." Hannah's voice faded as she and her companion rounded the corner.

Beth shook her head and turned to Tom, a smile on her face. "I'm not sure a musical career is right for those two. They could take their comedy act on the road and make a real killing."

Tom grinned. "Definitely. Jack loves to play dumb just to egg her on, but she falls for it every time. It's been going on for years."

Beth had the feeling something more had recently developed between their friends, but she kept that thought to herself. There was no need to start rumors, and she had her own personal life to worry about.

"You still want to eat, right?" Tom's hand slid down to take hers, leaving a trail of tingling flesh in its wake.

"Yes, of course." The muffin she'd had for breakfast, along with the snacks consumed during the day, wasn't enough to keep her going. Between all the walking they'd done today and the strenuous activities they'd engaged in last night, she'd probably lost a couple pounds.

Tom led her back out the main doors. "I wanted to go somewhere fancy, but now that we got ditched, I don't feel comfortable riding around a strange city, just the two of us." He pulled her to a stop, then gently lifted her chin. "Your safety is the most important thing to me, understand?"

Beth nodded, a lump in her throat. He was such a caring man. She missed him already, and they still had a week to go before she left.

"Good." Tom took a quick look around and pointed to a nearby family-style restaurant. "How does that one look to you? It's close enough to get someone from the crew if we need 'em."

She ignored his reminder of possible danger. "Hey, if it's got food, it works for me."

Minutes later, they were seated in a corner booth, water glasses filled and menus placed before them. Beth quickly made her selection and then leaned back to study Tom.

Throughout the ups and downs of the day, he had been at her side. She understood his attention was mostly because of Eric's threat, but she knew there were other reasons. She had her reasons for being with him, too, and none of them were because she wanted a bodyguard.

In the past twenty-four hours, he'd assumed the roles of friend, lover, and protector—and she honestly adored all those sides of him. But now, Beth wanted to know even more about this man who had captured her heart. Had he always possessed such a morally upright, appealing personality?

After placing their orders—pot roast for him, a chef salad for her, and beer for both—she asked, "What was it you told me in Jacksonville? That you and Leo had been friends since high school?" He nodded. "Tell me about it. How did you two meet?"

A wide grin spread across Tom's face. "Actually, it is a pretty funny story."

It turned out that Leo hadn't always been the picture-perfect front man he was now. He'd had quite a few physical problems when Tom met him.

"Are you serious? He was chubby and wore glasses?" Beth paused as the waitress returned with their beers. "I can't imagine that. He's hot!" Beth took a sip of her drink.

Tom plastered a mock frown on his face. "Not hotter than me, I hope."

She reached across the table to patronizingly pat his hand. "Of course not, sweetie. You're hot, too."

"Humph." Tom took a swallow from his glass, too. She'd badgered him into ordering the beer, saying one drink wouldn't compromise her safety. Finally he'd given in. "Anyway, I didn't tell you the best part yet."

"Oh, there's more? I can't wait to razz him about this tomorrow."

"No! Don't you dare. He'd kill me if he knew I told you."

She leered. "Even better. I can save it to blackmail you later." Except there wouldn't be a later for the two of them. This was as far as it could go.

Beth took a large gulp of beer and promptly choked.

"Whoa, sweetheart, are you okay?" Tom stood up, ready to run to her rescue. She waved him back into his seat.

"I'm fine." She cleared her throat a final time. "Now, tell me the rest."

He waited a brief moment, watching her. Only when she nodded and gestured to him did he continue on. "You know how Leo keeps his hair short? Well, it wasn't always like that."

"So?"

"So, his hair is really curly, and in high school he grew it out."

Beth began to smile.

"Right. Think big blonde Afro."

She laughed. "Seriously?"

"Yup. And on top of all those issues, he was smart. Still is, of course, but he has the music to take the edge off, so to speak. Back then, he was a bona fide nerd."

"And what, you were the golden boy?"

Their food arrived, and Tom waited until they were alone again before responding.

"Hardly. We were both lowly freshmen so it's not like I had any pull. I just didn't stand out as much as he did."

Beth swallowed her bite of salad with difficulty. "Leo was picked on?"

"The very first day he transferred in." Tom leisurely ate a couple spoonfuls of mashed potatoes.

"And?"

"And the next day he wasn't picked on." He smiled as he speared a piece of meat.

Beth gave up eating until his story was over. "What did you do? Beat up the bullies?"

"Nah. It was just harder for them to harass more than one person at a time, and I stuck to Leo like glue." He consumed another bite of his meal before continuing. "Eventually they left us alone."

So it turned out he'd always been a superhero after all. She'd thought that was the case. "And you guys lived through the rest of your high school existence in peace, right?"

"Not exactly."

When her stomach growled—loudly—Beth picked up her fork again. He apparently wanted to prolong the sordid tale, but there was no sense in her starving to death while he did it.

"You see, with his wacky hairstyle, Leo earned a nickname. Leo the Lion. Original, huh?" Tom downed another swallow of beer. "And since I'd entered the picture, I got one, too. Tommy the Tiger, I guess because I defended Leo so hard."

Beth's eyes misted, and she quickly looked down, blinking rapidly to clear them. "You guys had those nicknames all through high school?" She'd never imagined a normal teenage life could be so tough.

"Sort of. The badass seniors were gone after that first year, and, by then, we'd turned the names to our advantage."

"How's that?"

"We'd joined band as freshmen and fallen in love with performing. We knew back then we were going to be successful musicians or die trying." He ate a couple more bites before continuing. "That was the year I taught myself guitar. I taught Leo, too, and we both took piano lessons. Of course, we didn't broadcast that information around school." He winked and offered a crooked smile. "We didn't want to provide even more amusement for others."

"How can you laugh about this?" Beth could contain her disgust no longer. "It makes me sick to hear how you guys were treated! If only those jerks could see you two now, how handsome and successful you are. They'd be falling all over themselves to apologize. They'd—"

"Beth," Tom interrupted, "it's all right." He reached over to take her hand, squeezing it gently. "It was a long time ago, and things changed."

"Uh-huh." She wasn't happy with what he'd said, but she loved his familiar touch.

"No, really. You know that saying, 'What doesn't kill you only makes you stronger'? It's true. Or at least it was in our case."

"Excuse me, aren't you Tom Crowley? From Roadhouse?"

Beth pulled her hand away and turned to see a pair of pre-teen girls standing next to the table. They wore similar styles of summer clothing—one in pink, the other in yellow—and each sported two long blonde braids and a wide smile. Cute as buttons, either they were sisters or extremely close friends.

The one with braces spoke again. "It is you! I knew it!"

Tom graced the children with a warm smile. "Hello, ladies. What can I do for you?"

A brief bout of giggling and whispering occurred before the second girl asked, "Could we have your autograph, please?" She produced a pen and heart-shaped pad of paper from the small Barbie-themed purse hanging around her neck.

Tom immediately reached for the items. "Certainly you can have my autograph. One for each of you?" He looked from one grinning face to the other, both girls nodding so hard Beth was afraid their heads would snap off.

"I'm Amanda," said the Barbie fan. "And this is my sister,

Emily."

The smaller girl gave a quick wave. "Hi."

"Well, Amanda and Emily, it was very nice meeting both of you." Tom finished writing but hesitated before handing the pen and paper back. He tilted his head toward Beth. "This is Beth. She sings with Roadhouse, too, so do you want her to write something?" He flashed a teasing smile her way.

Oh, geez. "Tom, no—"

"Girls!" A harried-looking woman came down the aisle, her arms full with a purse, diaper bag, and restless infant. "What are you doing bothering these people—oh!"

She'd just gotten a close look at Tom. "Oh. My. God."

"Mommy! Mommy, I was right! It is Tom!" Emily jumped up and down and tugged on her mother's arm as she spoke. "And he gave us autographs, too! Look!" She pointed to the items Tom was returning to Amanda.

The woman stopped staring at Tom long enough to look down at her daughters. "I'll look later, Emily, but I think you two have bothered Mr. Crowley enough for today. Let's let him eat his dinner." Her apologetic glance encompassed Beth, too. "Sorry about this. They're really big fans of your band—I am, too—but we couldn't get to the show last night. Birthday party at the in-law's house." She rolled her eyes, indicating her opinion of the event.

Her baby fussed a little more, and the woman turned to leave. "Thanks again, and sorry about the interruption."

"Not a problem, ma'am. It's always nice to meet young fans. And they were very polite, too, weren't you, girls?"

His comment caused another flurry of giggles to erupt, but the woman still managed to get her young daughters heading toward the door. Amid waves and cries of "Thank you" and "Goodbye," they heard the mother chastising her children.

"Don't ever do something like that again! You were supposed to be using the bathroom, that's all. You're both lucky it really was Tom Crowley and not some weirdo. Just wait until I tell your father what you did …"

•

Tom couldn't stop smiling as he watched the family move away. Those girls were adorable.

"She was wrong."

He turned back to Beth. "Hmm? Wrong about what?"

"Little does that poor woman know, but you truly are a weirdo."

"Only about you, sweetheart." He reached for his beer. "But she was right to scold them. I'd do the same to my kids if they ever wandered off." And the instant he'd seen the girls, thoughts of having a family of his own had sprung to mind. They'd looked like miniature versions of Bethany, and his desire to get a commitment from her—soon—had flared up again.

Beth picked up her fork and stabbed some more of her salad. "You were very good with those girls. I'm impressed."

"I love kids." He, too, returned to his meal. "The fact that they were fans was just a bonus. They helped Roadhouse get where we are today."

Beth instantly waved her hand back and forth. "Wait, wait. You can't skip ahead like that. You were talking about high school. The awful nicknames, remember?"

"Oh, yeah." It was an integral part of who he was today, not likely to be forgotten. "See, Leo and I used to use the school's practice rooms after school. There was a sign-up list posted in the hallway. But whenever we'd put our names down in the morning, some jerk would cross them out and put our nicknames. At one point, somebody got too lazy to write 'the Tiger' and 'the Lion' and just wrote 'the Cats.'"

"I don't see this getting any better yet," Beth said dryly.

"It did. Trust me. Our band teacher knew what we were doing, and he suggested we hook up with some other guys he knew. They didn't play in the school band, but I think Mr. Seibert wanted to give them a reason to stay in school. And it worked. Normally we all wouldn't have hung out, but our music brought us together."

"And this relates to bullies and nicknames how?"

Tom laughed. "Turns out we were lazy, too. On the sign-up list, we didn't feel like writing all five of our names, so Leo just wrote 'the Cats,' figuring everyone would know who we were. But Manny, he said that was too wimpy. He changed it to 'the Wildcats,' and that's what we were called from then on."

Beth reclined against the high back of the booth and pushed a stray lock of hair behind her ear. "So your freshman nicknames led to your forming a band called the Wildcats."

"Yup, that about covers it."

Over the remainder of dinner Tom explained how his and Leo's first band gained popularity not as a bunch of geeks but as a group of really talented musicians. They won school and citywide awards and were invited to play at numerous public functions, despite the fact that the band members often changed.

"We definitely owe a lot to Manny, Frank, and Chris," Tom said, giving credit to the original guys they'd formed Wildcats with. "But they eventually went their own ways over the years."

"Did they quit school like the band teacher thought they would?"

"Frank did, but the others decided to put more effort into their classes so they could graduate on time."

"That's good."

"Yeah, but Leo and I could afford to split our time between academics and music, and we definitely didn't want to give up the band."

"So what'd you do?"

The waitress stopped by to clear their plates, and they decided to have coffee and share a dessert. When the steaming mugs and single dish of rich strawberry shortcake were in front of them, Tom answered Beth's question.

"We stuck it out together." He watched as Bethany swallowed a spoonful of the cream-covered confection and had to clear his throat before continuing. "Sometimes there were four Wildcats, sometimes five, but there were never less than two."

A spot of whipped topping remained on her bottom lip, tempting him to lick it off. Then her tongue slipped out to get it, and that drove him just as crazy.

"It must've been wonderful having such a great friend. Someone who was there through both good and bad times." Her wistful tone escaped his notice as Beth reached for another taste of berries and cream.

Her action kept his focus locked on her mouth, bringing to mind what she'd done with that mouth that very morning...

The only excuse for what Tom said next was that a desire-induced fog had replaced all rational thought.

"Leo was my best friend back then, and still is. That's why I want him to be best man at our wedding."

Chapter Fourteen

Damn it! Regret instantly filled Tom. Once again, he'd let important words fly without a drop of finesse.

He hurried to salvage the moment and erase the deer-in-the-headlights expression from Beth's face. "Sorry. Let me try that again."

Tom took her hand in his and lifted it to his lips for a gentle kiss. Staring intently into her eyes, he asked, "Bethany Miller, will you marry me? Please?"

She squeezed her eyes shut and remained silent for a minute.

It was the longest minute of his life.

Finally, she pressed her lips together and opened her eyes. What he saw in the blue depths wasn't what he'd expected, and he knew what he'd hear before she even said the words.

"I'm sorry, Tom, but I can't. I can't marry you."

She pulled her hand away and lowered her gaze, not adding a bit of explanation.

And that pissed him off.

Yes, he was heartbroken, but now he was angry, too. Why the hell was she saying no to him?

And that's exactly what he asked. In nicer terms, of course, but only because they were in public. The restraint cost him dearly. "Why not?"

Her eyes flicked up for a second before skittering away again. "Tom, please."

But his irritation only grew. He kept his voice calm and level but left no doubt of his displeasure. "No. I want to know why you can't marry me. Because the only thing I understand is why you should. I love you and you love me. Isn't that enough?"

She didn't answer him but instead looked him in the eye and

asked a question of her own. "Do you remember when we first talked, that night at Gregory's?"

He nodded. He'd been intrigued by her right from the start and only more so after they'd shared a few drinks at the bar.

"You brought up the song 'Beth' and said what a great song it was."

"Yeah, so what?"

"I don't want that to be my life. I don't want to be that Beth, sitting around when you're gone. And I definitely don't want to be on the road most of the year like when I was younger."

Scenes of his own adolescence flashed through Tom's mind like a slide show: His mother warning him of the unreliability of a musician's life. Him trying to convince her he could make anything work if he wanted it bad enough.

As the dinner he'd consumed rolled around in his stomach, Tom prayed he'd been right.

"It sounds like you've been thinking about this a while."

Her gaze dropped again, and she fidgeted with her silverware. "I guess I have."

He figured he might as well get it all out in the open. "So you're saying the only way you'll marry me is if I quit the band?"

"No!" Her eyes shot back to his. "I would never ask that of you. I know how much you love what you do."

"Then what do you want me to do?" Frustration made his voice louder, causing nearby diners to glance his way. Tom struggled to stay in control. And, once again, he reached for Bethany's hand. "I love you and I love music," he said quietly. "So why are you asking me to choose?"

A single tear rolled down her cheek. "I'm not. I'm making the choice for you."

Tom could feel a muscle twitching in his jaw. "I'm not stupid, you know. Roadhouse's popularity could last five years or it could be over next week. There's no way to tell how long the ride will last, but it definitely won't be forever."

He squeezed her hand tighter and reached over to wipe a second tear from her silken skin. "But understand this, sweetheart. I know, in my heart, that we can last forever." He held her gaze, allowing her to see his soul, if she chose. "Don't you believe that?"

"I want to," Beth whispered. She sniffed and roughly wiped the wetness from her face. "But honestly, Tom," she continued hoarsely, "we haven't known each other all that long. I knew Eric a lot longer, I thought I knew everything about him, and look what happened."

Tom slammed a fist on the table. "I'm not Eric!"

"I know that!" She laid a warm hand over his clenched one. "I know you'd never intentionally hurt me like he did. But things would change between us just the same, and I don't think I could stand it when that happened."

He tried once more to persuade her. "I trust my feelings and I trust you. But how can I get you to trust me? What do I have to do?"

Beth unexpectedly pulled her hands away and stood up. She shook her head. "It's not you at all, Tom. It's me I don't trust."

She spun away and headed for the exit.

Fearing for her safety, Tom quickly threw enough bills on the table to cover the meal and a generous tip. As he rushed to follow Beth, his heart thudded heavily in his chest.

It looked like his mother may have been right after all: Music and a family don't mix.

•

Eyes closed, Beth sat curled up in one of the tour bus seats and pretended to be napping. After all that had happened lately, she needed some time to herself.

Most shocking of all had been Tom's proposal of marriage. She knew she hadn't explained herself very well to him, but she'd been overwhelmed with emotions.

Love for Tom. Desire to say yes. And fear. Fear that the future would be a rerun of her past.

That feeling had filled her the most, to the point of panic. She'd had to leave the restaurant or risk a total meltdown.

Luck had been with her: She'd managed to cross the street right before the traffic light changed, and the elevator doors had closed behind her just as Tom entered the hotel lobby.

She'd spent the rest of the night alone in her room. Hannah hadn't poked and prodded about what was wrong but instead gave Beth her cell number as she left, directing her to call if she wanted to talk.

Beth hadn't called.

She'd lain in her freshly made bed and watched a sappy old love story on HBO. With tears rolling down her face and her shoulders heaving with quiet sobs, she hugged the extra pillow, swearing she could still smell Tom on it.

Exhaustion must have claimed her because the next she knew it was morning, and Hannah was shaking her awake. They had to pack up and get on the road to Syracuse.

She and Tom exchanged little more than a nod and "Good morning" during breakfast, and, feeling very awkward amidst the others' liveliness, Beth had been happy to have the meal over with.

Now, as they traveled east along Interstate 90, she could hear Tom's voice farther back in the bus where he sat playing cards with some of the guys. Meanwhile, Hannah still silently perused the magazine she'd taken out earlier—it contained the latest fashion trends, no doubt.

At the last minute her father had decided to ride on the band's bus to New York, and he sat on a couch a few feet away, talking with Dylan.

Why the change, Beth wasn't certain. There was no reason to think that one of the band member's had told him about the nasty package she'd received, so maybe he'd just wanted a break from the road crew.

As Beth shifted position, trying to get more comfortable in the padded seat, George's words caught her attention.

"I love traveling. It's one of the reasons I've stayed in the business so long. Always seeing new places, meeting new people. But New England was one of the areas I liked the best, especially in the fall. The foliage was beautiful."

Her father liked watching leaves change color? That was news to her.

"Fall was nice, but winter was the best," Dylan replied. "Snowmobiling and skiing—that's what I'd be doing if there was snow on the ground. And if there wasn't any in New York, there were a lot of resorts in Vermont that stayed prepared."

"A real outdoorsman, are you?"

"Oh, yeah. I love it all. Georgia may not have the snow, but there's still plenty to do. And I come back to New York to visit family pretty often. It's funny how most of my visits happen during ski season, though. Very strange."

Beth's mouth twitched in response to the wry humor in Dylan's voice, but her father chuckled out loud. "Works out good for everyone, eh? Your folks get to see you, and you get to hit the slopes."

"Yup. It's a perfect solution. I've always been big on thinking things through. Less aggravation in the end."

Hmm. She never would've pictured a guy like Dylan to be big on planning. He looked more like the flies-by-the-seat-of-his-pants type.

Beth shamelessly tuned back in to the men's conversation when she heard her name mentioned.

"I'll never forget when I took Bethany skiing for the first time. It was hard not to laugh, but I held it in because I knew she didn't think it was funny. She was only seven or eight years old at the time."

"What happened?"

As her father told Dylan the tale of her first skiing experience, Beth let the memories resurface.

"I was working a four month winter tour for a rock band, and Beth had just come to live with me in late summer. The schedule had a couple of stops in Colorado, so on an off-day I decided to introduce my daughter to the joys of downhill skiing."

Now Dylan was the one to laugh. "Uh-oh. That sounds ominous."

"No, no. Nothing really bad happened. It just took a while to actually get to the skiing part."

Beth cracked her eyes open, wanting to see George's face as he spoke. Would he really describe the day the same way she remembered it?

At that moment her father turned to look at her, a smile on his weathered face. It broadened into a grin when he saw she was awake. "Remember that day, Bethany? When I took you to the bunny slope for the first time?"

Beth nodded but remained silent. She glanced around the bus and saw he'd gained additional listeners with his loud voice. Leo, Sam, Jack, and Hannah were all looking at her father, waiting for him to continue.

Tom, however, kept his eyes on her. She could still feel the heat of his gaze long after she dropped her own, too emotionally weary to act defiant.

"Beth was a sensitive little girl," her father was saying. "She'd see a baby crying and she'd want to comfort it. Same with puppies and kittens. She didn't want to see anybody in distress."

George looked her way once more. "She's still like that. Don't let her tell you otherwise." He turned back to Dylan. "But, anyway, I'd told Bethany that we were going to the bunny slope so she could get her first lesson, and she started crying. I thought she was mad she couldn't go on the big runs, but that wasn't it."

Beth could picture it like it was yesterday. Yet another moment of discontent in her upbringing with her and George not seeing eye to eye.

"She was sobbing and screaming that she didn't want to go, and I didn't understand why. She'd been so excited to try skiing when we first got to the mountain." George shook his head. "I swear, people probably thought I was beating the poor child."

Beth could feel everybody's eyes on her, and she tried to curl up tighter into her seat. When her father finished this story, they'd all think she was nuts.

"So what was the problem?" Hannah asked, her magazine lying, temporarily forgotten, across her lap.

George looked to Beth once again, this time with a raised eyebrow. Should I tell them?

She shrugged her shoulders in response. Go ahead. You may as well finish.

But Tom was the one who spoke next. "Beth thought there were rabbits on the bunny slope, and she didn't want to hurt them. Is that it?"

She snapped her head around to stare at him, her mouth agape. Then her gaze shot to her father, who insisted, "I didn't tell him, honey. I swear."

Beth looked back to Tom, disbelieving. "Lucky guess."

He slowly shook his head, his dark gaze locked with hers as he mouthed, "I know you." At the same time Jack said, "He was right? That's too weird."

"Yeah, but that's exactly how it was," George answered. "But once she calmed down and I showed her the hill, Beth was fine."

"So you ended up having fun that day?" Dylan, the ski enthusiast, just had to ask her that. And Tom, of course, kept watching her, waiting for her reply.

Beth thought long and hard before answering. She'd always remembered that day as one more time when her father didn't understand her, didn't want her around because she interfered with his fun.

But now she forced herself to objectively picture what happened on the mountain.

Yes, she'd been upset. She'd been a child—one who had never skied before and had a vivid imagination.

Yet her father had not laughed at her. He hadn't tried to hurry her along or force her to the slope against her will.

Instead, he had sat down next to her and hugged her while she cried. And when she'd finally explained why she was upset, George had calmly pointed to the beginner's slope from the window of the lodge and let her make up her own mind about going outside.

Her father had been loving and supportive, and it had turned out to be one of the best days of her life.

Beth doubted she'd ever thanked her father for it before, but there was no time like the present. "I had a terrific time." She looked her father in the eye. "Thank you, daddy. It was fun."

To everyone else her statement may have sounded completely ordinary, but, to Beth, it was momentous. By saying those words aloud, she had admitted to herself that her childhood might not have been the nightmare she kept proclaiming it was.

"You're welcome, honey." George winked and then resumed talking to Dylan, this time in a quieter voice.

The rustling noises behind her indicated the others also had gone back to their previous activities. But Beth sensed that one person remained unmoving. Watching her.

She carefully turned her head to meet Tom's gaze. From the look in his eyes, she knew he'd realized that part of her defenses were in shambles.

And if he pushed hard enough, the rest would come tumbling down, too, leaving her with no willpower to say no to him.

•

Syracuse stirred up a mix of emotions in Tom.

As usual, performing raised him to a high no drug could ever hope to match. And, due to the hard work of the crew, the show had once again gone smoothly.

But the feelings aroused by Beth—love, concern, frustration—did their best to douse the excitement of the concert. Tom could feel the internal struggle throughout his performance, and he fought hard not to let it show.

By the crowd's enthusiastic reaction, he thought he'd pulled it off. But now, at the post-concert autograph session, Tom discovered he hadn't been able to hide his feelings well enough.

"You gotta snap out of it, man," Leo said in a low voice. Fans were lined up, waiting for the band to sign their programs and other assorted merchandise. Any minute the security guards would allow them to file past the long tables to briefly chat with the performers.

Tom figured this really wasn't a good time for Leo to bring up personal issues. "I'm fine, Leo. Let it be."

"I can't. All our asses are on the line, not just yours. We've worked too hard to blow it now."

The first of the crowd, two teenage boys, approached the other end of the table where Beth and Hannah were seated.

"Nothing's going to get blown, Leo. The show went well, and the audience loved us."

Beth's face lit up as she spoke to the boys and signed their programs. She and Hannah even posed for a picture with the teens before the guards prompted them to keep the line moving. God, she was beautiful.

A rough shake of Tom's left shoulder pulled his focus from Beth. "What the hell?"

"You may have done well enough on stage tonight, but you're screwing up royally right now. You haven't stopped staring at Beth since we've sat down, and it's gotta stop. I don't know what went on between the two of you, and I don't want to know. But none of these people need to know, either. They have to come first right now. Got it?"

Tom had never seen his friend so angry before. "You're right. This isn't the time or the place."

As the line of high-spirited fans reached their end of the table, Tom purposefully shoved all thoughts of Beth out of his mind. Young, old, black, white, male, female—Roadhouse's great variety of supporters served to distract him with their jokes, compliments, and questions.

But toward the end of the long night, as the final stragglers made their way along the table, images of Bethany crept back in.

Her voice, her laughter—without even looking her way, he was constantly reminded of how much he wanted her. How much he loved her.

There was absolutely no way he could let her go.

"Oh, no. You've got that glazed look in your eyes again. Can't you hold on just a few more minutes?"

He turned to Leo. "I love Beth, and I asked her to marry me."

Hazel eyes widened. "What did she say?"

Wham! The men jumped as a tour program was slammed down on the table in front of Tom. He raised his gaze to look into the narrowed eyes of a young, dark-haired woman.

She was clearly upset, so he quickly pasted a wide smile on his face and tried to smooth things over. "Sorry, ma'am. How are you tonight?"

As Tom scribbled a greeting across a page of the souvenir book, he asked the same general questions he'd asked other fans. How'd you like the show? What did you like the best? What's your favorite Roadhouse song?

Any answers he obtained could be used to make future concerts better. But, of course, it only helped if he actually listened to the answers given, and this time he didn't. His mind was busy running through scenarios of how to convince Bethany they belonged together.

"Nice meeting you," he said, trying not to be rude but wanting to get this night over with. He slid the girl's program over to Leo and turned to the last two people in line—a middle-aged couple wearing matching white concert tees, jeans, and brown cowboy hats.

He soon learned the pair lived in Tennessee but were in New York visiting friends. They'd heard about the concert at the last minute and had abandoned their hosts for the night because the wife was such an admirer of the band.

"And if Jessie wants to do something, we do it. Right, sugarplum?"

While her husband looked on with an indulgent smile, Tom carefully signed Jessie's T-shirt across her slightly rotund abdomen.

"I hope the show was worth all the trouble you went to."

"Oh, it was fantastic!" Jessie said. "Even Bob was dancing around, and, trust me, that doesn't happen much. It's quite the sight!" She laughed and nudged her husband in the side. He responded by lifting her in a big bear hug and planting a loud smooch on her bright red lips.

"Oh, Bobby, now quit it." Jessie playfully slapped Bob's chest before turning back to pick up her autographed program from Leo. "Save it for later, sweetie, when we don't have an audience."

Tom and Leo burst out laughing when their outspoken fan winked at them and slid an arm through her husband's. "Tootles, boys! Keep up the great work!"

The woman waved bejeweled fingers at them as the twosome moved away. Tom just shook his head and laughed harder when he saw Bob's hand slide down to squeeze his wife's ample rear end.

The couple had been very sweet, and the way they'd interacted with one another had made Tom envious. That's what he wanted with Beth. For as long as he lived, he wanted her by his side. He wanted to dote on her, treasure her, do anything he could to make her happy. He'd shout his feelings from the rooftop if he had to, just to convince her they could make it—together.

Wait a minute.

"So what'd she say when you proposed?"

Tom looked back to Leo, his mind still tossing the idea around. It just might work. "She said no. But it doesn't matter."

"I think if the woman turned you down, it matters."

The band members pushed their chairs back and stood, preparing to leave the Landmark Theatre for the night.

"You just have to move on, buddy. Even if you don't want to." Leo clamped a strong hand on Tom's shoulder. "Sorry."

"No, Leo." Tom shook off his friend's grip. "It's not over. I'm not letting her go." His gaze followed Bethany as she led the rest of Roadhouse, heading out behind the security guards.

As the group moved past a few fans lingering near the backstage doors, Tom caught sight of the brunette he'd inadvertently irritated minutes earlier. He threw a cheery wave and smile in her direction, hoping to eradicate any bad feelings she might still harbor. Roadhouse didn't need anyone speaking ill of its members at this stage of the game.

Moving into the backstage area, Tom immediately resumed his quiet conversation with Leo. "I think I know how to win Beth over. But I'll need everybody's help to do it."

◆

Beth was preparing to go on stage at Albany's Palace Theatre when Hannah walked into their shared dressing room. "Here." She handed Beth a sheet of paper. "It's the set list for tonight's show. The guys wanted to do something a little different and switched up a couple of songs."

Beth looked over the list. From what she could see, the only song that was out of its usual order was "Dandelions." It was now the last song of the night. "Why the change?" she asked Hannah.

The other woman shrugged. "You'd have to ask them that. I just do what I'm told." She sliced a chunk of cheddar from the block on a nearby snack tray and popped it in her mouth.

Beth studied Hannah's expression. In the short time she'd known her, the redhead had never seemed the meek type.

"Twenty minutes 'til show time!" came the call through the backstage area.

As Hannah took a seat next to her at the vanity, Beth continued applying her stage make-up and let her suspicions fade away. It wasn't really a big deal, anyway. Since "Dandelions" was currently in the top ten of both the Pop and Country charts, the men had probably decided to emphasize its success by playing it as the final song of their concert tour.

The thought made her hand shake, and she quickly wiped off the spot of mascara that landed beside her eye.

Tomorrow would be the last she'd see of Tom, and she had no one to blame but herself. Not because she hadn't accepted his marriage proposal—that would've only led to heartache for both of them—but for not having the courage to believe in their love in the first place.

No matter how strong her feelings were for Tom—and she loved him with all her heart—she was convinced she would eventually do something that would push him away for good.

Best case scenario? She'd make his life miserable because her dislike of life on the road was so deeply ingrained.

But what she'd told Tom the other night had been the honest truth: She would never ask him to quit the band or stop performing.

Music was his life, and his hard work and dedication to the craft made her love him all the more.

So until she could get over what he did for a living, or at least make peace with it, she had to leave. There was no telling when, or if, this crucial revelation would occur, and she had no right to ask Tom to wait until it did.

He had to do what he had to do, and so did she.

Beth let out a deep breath and took a last look at herself in the mirror. Her fancy make-up and relaxed hairstyle had her looking calm and collected, but she knew inside that she was barely hanging on.

Tough cookies. Get out there and give it everything you've got. For Tom.

Widening her eyes and blinking to clear the moisture that had welled up, Beth stood. "Ready?" she asked.

"Yup. I'm good to go." Hannah stood and made a final adjustment to the bodice of her snug black dress. "Let's do it, sweetie."

Forcing a bright smile to her face, Beth headed out to sing for her lover for the last time.

•

Music was a balm for any weary soul. It could either lift a person out of the doldrums or comfort him if there was no other solace to be had.

Halfway through the first song, Beth no longer had to pretend she was enjoying herself. The band's energy spread throughout the theatre, to every audience member and back to her. She knew no matter what the future held for her and Tom, she'd never forget being a part of this experience. Having worked as both a roadie and a singer, the past five weeks on the road would leave behind nothing but fond memories.

She'd made some good friends, and she'd fallen in love with a great guy. Even made some money to boot.

And the best news of all had come mere seconds before Roadhouse took the stage, when they'd been informed that Eric Sharpe had been captured in Las Vegas.

Beth had been right about him. He hadn't the slightest interest in taking revenge on her. He may have spared the time to send her a nasty bouquet, but that was the extent of his malevolence.

It seemed Eric would rather use his precious free time to gamble and visit strip clubs.

So Beth was worry-free for the moment and able to totally immerse herself in the excitement of performing. Everyone on stage added something unique to the show, and although she knew she wasn't a great talent, Beth hoped she complemented the others in some way. From the audience's reaction, they loved everything they saw and heard.

Intermission came and went too fast for Beth. Between using the bathroom and fixing her make-up, she had no time to talk to the men. With tomorrow being the Fourth of July, some of them were departing right after the autograph session to visit relatives over the long weekend, and she didn't know if she'd have time to properly say goodbye.

For all the complaining she'd done about traveling, and she'd complained a lot, one would think she'd be happy the tour was ending. But, instead, she dreaded its close.

She was really going to miss these guys. Tom the most, of course, but all the men and women she'd met had become her friends, and San Francisco didn't seem quite so appealing anymore.

"Don't forget about the set change," Hannah reminded her as they exited their dressing room for the second time.

"Oh. Right." Beth's attention drifted as the men emerged from their nearby rooms. Her eyes searched for and found Tom in the narrow hallway.

No doubt the man could wear a paper bag and still look hot.

But, right now, in his informal outfit of faded blue jeans, black T-shirt, and sneakers, he looked like your friendly neighborhood blue-collar worker. Yummy.

His dark gaze locked with hers, and Beth almost looked away, unwilling to see the hurt in his eyes from what she'd done. But then, of all things, he winked.

Here she was, thinking she'd broken his heart, and he just smiled that sexy smile of his and winked at her.

Then he turned away and headed back toward the stage area.

"Are you done catching flies? Can we go now?" Hannah waved her hand in front of Beth's face.

Beth immediately pressed her lips together in a tight smile. "Sure. Let's get this done."

They followed the men down the stairs, and minutes later

the curtains parted. The crowd welcomed Roadhouse back with rousing cheers.

Once again Beth surrendered to the music. And when Leo introduced the band members for the final time this tour, she soaked up the applause her name elicited.

She knew she would never again perform in surroundings like this, but she had to admit the fans' attention and appreciation could easily become addictive. And for the introverted person she normally was, that was saying a lot.

Finally it was time for the last song. Beth expected "Dandelions" to be played in its normal, mellow manner. After all, it was a ballad and required no loud accompaniment.

But she was still quite surprised when Leo walked offstage to grab two wooden stools from behind the drapes. As the singer made his way back to center stage, Tom began to speak into his microphone.

"How are ya'll doin' tonight? You havin' fun?"

Each of his questions was greeted with loud cheers and whistles.

"Thanks, man," he said to Leo as a stool was placed beside him. Then he slid the strap of his electric guitar over his shoulder and set the instrument in a stand to his right, quickly replacing it with an acoustic six-string. The audience quieted down as he began playing a few chords.

This was not the usual approach to performing "Dandelions." Beth glanced at Hannah, curious to know what was happening. But the other woman remained looking forward as Tom continued on.

"I hope you guys don't mind if we do something a little different tonight. Something which has never been done before and, hopefully, won't need to be done again."

Beth was lost. What the heck was going on? And how come no one else on stage seemed in the least concerned about Tom's little speech?

In fact, Leo had picked up his own acoustic guitar, and both he and Tom had taken up positions on the stools. All the other men had relaxed poses, and another glance at Hannah showed her trying to suppress a smile. Or maybe it was a laugh.

Because Beth sure felt the joke was on her.

"This is a song I started to write back in college, and I worked all the bugs out of it last year." The soft music coming from Tom and Leo's instruments created a warm, inviting atmosphere. The audience remained silent as Tom spoke, undoubtedly impatient to find out what he had in store for them.

Beth was dying to know, too.

"Normally Leo sings this song, but I asked my friends here on stage with me if I could sing it tonight. And they said okay." A brief outburst of encouraging applause and shouts rang out, but quickly died down as the men's soothing music became recognizable as the introduction to "Dandelions."

"'Dandelions' is about love, but I have to admit I didn't know squat about that emotion when I wrote the song. Sure, I loved my family and friends, but I didn't understand what it meant to love someone with all your heart. To want that person by your side for the rest of your life." He paused for a moment. "And now I do."

Another round of applause followed his words, and although the same bars of music kept being repeated, Tom played them harder, as though communicating his emotions through the song.

Meanwhile, Beth couldn't breathe. What the hell was he doing?

The music quieted, and Tom spoke into his mic once again. "It's been said that love is a many splendored thing, and I totally believe that. I know it's hard sometimes, and we've all gotten hurt at one point or another on the path to true love. But I also know it's all worth it in the end. Right?"

Beth could feel the stage vibrating beneath her feet, the audience's response was so loud. But again, the noise didn't linger very long.

"'Dandelions' is all about the possibilities that love brings to people, if they just let it. And tonight I want to dedicate this song to the woman I love." For the first time since intermission, Tom shifted to look directly at her. "This is for you, Beth."

Remaining sideways on his stool, Tom launched into the first verse of "Dandelions" with the audience's screaming and clapping drowning out most of his words.

Hannah nudged Beth to move forward on stage, but she stood frozen in place, really hearing the lyrics for the first time—and thankful this song didn't require her active participation. Tom's crooning and Leo's additional harmonizing vocals were all that was necessary.

"Dandelions aren't just weeds, they're symbols of what everyone needs. Spots of color in a sea of green—listen and you'll see what I mean."

His words washed over her, his voice deep and soothing to her ears. And to her heart.

He was making it so damn hard for her to leave...

"... love colors people's lives—love from friends, children, husbands, wives. Just like the flowers, love keeps coming back."

She was only released from Tom's hypnotic gaze when he began to play the more complicated bridge of the tune. And after that, she refused to look at him again.

Two emotions raged within her. Love tempted her to say yes to all Tom was offering. And anger wanted her to scream at him for embarrassing her like this.

"... love can make you high and dandelions can, too. Just let yourself be loved and everything will be fine. And out of those dandelions we'll make dandelion wine."

Obviously the rest of Roadhouse knew what Tom's plans had been. And they had all hidden their secret from her very well. Beth had no clue what was coming her way.

As Tom and Leo blended their voices for a final round of the song's chorus, Beth took an action of her own. Unwilling to risk another near-meltdown in public, and not caring how unprofessional she looked, she stepped down from the riser then crossed behind the black curtain hiding the rear stage area. Ignoring the startled crew members near the monitor at stage left, Beth headed back upstairs to her dressing room.

Where she got her second big surprise of the night.

Chapter Fifteen

Tom was torn. He'd seen Beth leave the stage and wanted to go after her, but he didn't want to upset his friends. Or the audience. Once again, he was forced to decide between personal and professional issues.

This really sucked.

He caught Leo's eye as the final strains of "Dandelions" faded into the crowd's enthusiastic applause.

"Go," his friend directed with a nod of his head. Then Leo leaned closer so he could be heard. "Go after her. We can handle this."

Tom didn't hesitate. After removing his guitar, he waved to the audience and gave a sweeping gesture of acknowledgement to the rest of the band. As he jogged offstage, Hannah and the guys launched into a semi-coordinated jam session often used to warm up during rehearsals.

In the wings, Tom handed his instrument to a nearby technician and then continued on toward the dressing rooms, desperate to locate Beth. He needed to know how she felt. And what exactly she wanted most in her life. Would she fight for him or against him?

He pounded once on the women's dressing room door and called, "Beth, I'm coming in!"

As the doorknob turned beneath his fingers, Tom heard a squeaking sound from within, like that of a tiny mouse. But he paid no attention to it—until he'd already entered the changing room and the door was shut behind him.

And by then it was too late.

This was so much worse than the spider and maggot-filled package. And so unexpected that his heart nearly stopped.

Beth stood in front of him, but she was not alone. Close beside her was a familiar-looking young woman, similar to Beth in height but slighter in build. The brunette was dressed in a red leather miniskirt and barely-there pink tank top.

It was an outfit meant to attract a man's attention, but the only thing Tom saw was the knife she was holding.

It was pressed against Bethany's tender throat, which lay exposed by her low-cut dress.

The woman's other hand was wound around Beth's long hair, keeping her trapped.

"Let her go." He kept his voice low and even. He had no idea what was happening, but he also had no intention of upsetting this psychopath. Not with Beth's life at risk.

"No, Tom! She took you away from me, and she can't do that! You were supposed to love me, not her!" A hard tug on Beth's hair emphasized the brunette's anger. And her instability.

After a quick look to verify she hadn't been cut, Tom's gaze slid up to catch Beth's. The fear he saw in her wide eyes was almost more than he could take.

Not sure what the intruder's reaction would be but needing to try anything to get Beth released, Tom explained, "I don't even know who you are."

Oops, wrong thing to say.

His remark resulted in another yank to Beth's scalp and a drop of blood appearing on her pale skin. Her chest rose and fell frantically as her breathing accelerated.

"Yes, you know me! I'm Casey!" was the screeching response. "Don't you remember?"

Another look at Beth's face revealed the pain she was in. Apparently Casey was stronger than she looked.

"That's right! Casey. Of course I remember you." Tom took a small step toward the women, willing to do whatever was necessary to save Beth from this lunatic.

"Stay back! I swear I'll hurt her." Casey moved two steps back, dragging Bethany with her. Her eyes narrowed as she gave further warning. "You'd better not be lying to me, Tom."

Tom held up his hands in, he hoped, a non-threatening manner. "I wouldn't lie to you, Casey." He took a chance. "I just didn't recognize you with your hair pulled back. It was down every other time I saw you."

Oh, please let that be true.

Casey's eyes brightened, and she gave Tom a wide smile. "You noticed! I wanted to look more sophisticated for you tonight. And up-dos are so much classier than this long mess, don't you think?" She gave yet another tug on Beth's hair, and her smile twisted into a devilish smirk.

"Maybe I should fix it. What do you think, a shaggy dog cut for a flea bag like her?" She moved the knife from Bethany's throat to her nape, and Tom saw his chance.

But as soon as he stepped forward, Casey swung her arm toward him. "Uh, uh. I love you, Tom, and I don't want to hurt you. But you're making this very hard."

Tom stood his ground, hoping to keep Casey's attention on him. "Then let's make it easy. Let her go and we can leave here. Together."

Her eyes widened. "You'd come with me? And forget all about her?"

Yeah, like that would ever happen, nutso.

"Casey, look at yourself. You're beautiful." And obviously narcissistic in addition to being insane, because she did what he instructed. She shifted position so her back was to the door and she could see her reflection in the vanity mirror.

But all along she kept a firm grip on Beth's hair and her weapon raised in mid-air. So Tom tried to distract her further. "And no other woman has tried so hard to get my attention, so I know you really do love me."

"Oh, yes. I do." Casey's eyes slid from the mirror to meet Tom's. "I've followed you this whole tour. And I watched you at the hardware store, too."

What? This girl had more problems than he'd thought.

"You were at my family's hardware store? In Georgia?" Hearing footsteps in the hallway outside, Tom raised his voice to cover the noise as best he could. "Why didn't you say hello to me, Casey? I would've talked to you. It didn't have to come to this."

Once again it was the wrong thing to say. Casey's brows immediately pulled together, and the overhead light glinted on the knife's short but sharp blade as she wagged it at him.

"You wouldn't have talked to me! You were too busy with that other woman before, in Savannah. And now this one's throwing herself at you like a common tramp!" This time her yank caused

Beth to cry out. "I've had it! You're mine, and you always will be!" Casey moved quickly, but it all felt like slow motion to Tom.

"No!" He lunged forward, grabbing for the girl's arm before her weapon could make its intended slice across Beth's throat.

At the same time, the door at Casey's back was pushed open, shoving her off balance—and into Tom.

•

As soon as her captor began to fall away and a knife was no longer aimed at her jugular, Beth twisted to get loose.

Minus a few hairs, she sidestepped the door as it swung open. "Watch out!" she yelled to whoever was entering.

"Beth, are you—oh my God! We need help!" Hannah's cries brought the sound of heavy footfalls on the stairs.

But Beth didn't wait for assistance. Instead, she grabbed a chair from in front of the vanity and swung it with all her might, knocking Casey away from Tom. A second blow caused the girl to drop her weapon, and Hannah finished her off with a right hook.

As Casey fell to the floor, Beth hurried to Tom's side and wrapped her shaky arms around him. She pressed her face into the warm curve of his neck, inhaling the musky scent of him. "Are you all right?"

He returned her embrace, hugging her so tightly she could hardly breathe. "I should be asking you that." She felt his lips brush against her temple. "But the way you took her out, I guess I know the answer already."

Beth tilted her head back to meet his gaze. "Trust me, it was the adrenaline," she answered as assorted band and crew members piled through the doorway and stumbled to a halt.

"Thanks for hurrying, guys," Hannah commented dryly. "Don't worry that little Miss Wacko here wanted to slice us up into sushi." With a motion of her hand she indicated both the dazed woman sprawled on the floor and the knife firmly held in place by the toe of her black shoe. "We handled it."

"What the hell happened here?" Jack demanded to know.

Hannah shrugged her shoulders and nodded toward Beth and Tom. "They know more than I do."

"She was in the room when I got here." Beth twisted in Tom's hold but kept an arm around his waist. "She grabbed me and threatened me with that knife. I think she took it off the snack tray."

Sam leaned over to wrap a handkerchief around the blade and pull it out of Casey's reach. "Did anyone call the police?"

"Already done, Sam." Mike held up his cell phone. "And George is going to make an announcement that the Meet and Greet is cancelled."

"No, don't do that." Tom's voice was insistent but somehow didn't sound quite right. "You guys need to see the fans. Security has this covered for now." He haphazardly waved his left arm toward the two uniformed men who were watching over a handcuffed Casey, now seated upright on the floor. "Beth and I will join you as soon as we're done talking to the police."

The more talking he did, the more slurred his speech became. And the heavier he felt against her side. "Tom, do you—"

Then Beth felt the warm liquid on her bare back for the first time. "Oh, God! He's been hurt!"

Leo and Dylan hurried to relieve her of Tom's weight, pushing him into a chair just as his knees gave out. Beth moved to see how badly he'd been cut, and she nearly got sick.

Tom's right arm was hanging loosely at his side, the forearm covered in blood. Like a scene from a horror movie, dark red liquid dripped from his fingertips and onto the floor. There was no way for her to tell how much damage had actually been done.

"Someone get a doctor!" she yelled, grabbing a clean hand towel from the vanity and wrapping it around Tom's arm.

He was getting so pale. And there was so much blood.

What if an artery had been cut? What if they couldn't stop the bleeding in time?

"Hurry!" she screamed.

•

He could smell her. The light berry scent of her soaps and lotions mingled with the antiseptic odor that prevailed in places like this.

Tom opened his eyes to find Beth sitting by the side of his hospital bed. He'd told the doctors in the emergency room that he didn't want to be admitted, but they'd insisted on keeping an eye on him for a few hours. A six-inch-long cut made by a dirtied paring knife wasn't something they wanted to ignore.

He'd been unable to talk to Beth while in the ER or during transit to this room. And, unfortunately, as soon as he'd been left alone, Tom had fallen asleep.

He must have napped for at least four or five hours, since it was now daylight. He could easily see Beth's pensive features in the dim light sneaking in between the vertical blinds. She was looking at the muted television hanging on the wall in front of his bed, but it was obvious she wasn't following the action on the screen. She wore a pale blue sleeveless top, denim shorts, and sandals, which meant she'd been able to return to the hotel after the attack last night.

Attack. God, how that word scared him. He'd almost lost her. Forever.

And because of what had happened, he knew—despite her put-together appearance—odds were she was a mess inside.

"Hi," he said softly, not wanting to startle her.

She jumped anyway. After quickly using the remote to turn off the TV, she turned to face him.

He saw right away that her face bore traces of the previous night's incident. There were circles under her eyes, and her lips trembled so much she could hardly form a token smile.

"Oh, good. You're awake. The nurse said to let you sleep as long as you wanted. That your body needed help to recover from the shock it received." She teared up and her smile faltered, but she promptly leaned over to kiss his brow, not letting him see her distress. When she sat back in the chair, her composure was back in place.

"Are you ready to hear the whole story? The deal with Casey the nutjob?"

Tom cautiously nodded his head. "Only if you want to tell me." He didn't want anything else to upset Beth. She'd been through enough hell in her life, especially in the last week. But she curled her long legs beneath her, rested her chin in her hand, and began to speak briskly, as though the entire incident was something she'd heard about on the nightly news.

"Her real name is Cassiopeia Sommersby—geez, with a name like that, who wouldn't go crazy?" She shook her head and waved her hand back and forth. "But, anyway, her father is some super-rich corporate shark based outside of Savannah, and her mother is your stereotypical socialite—busy with shopping and looking good. Oh, and Casey's being transferred from the Albany County

Jail to a private mental hospital. Daddy dearest probably wants to keep this whole mess quiet, but too bad. It'll all come out when the trial begins."

Trial? Tom wasn't sure how to say this. "Are you sure you wouldn't rather settle this out of court? I mean, you've already been through one traumatic experience, testifying at Eric's trial."

He wished she would come closer. He wanted her to touch him again. And he wanted to touch her. Badly.

But she continued to sit in the chair, an odd expression on her face.

"If you don't want to go through that again, I'm fine with it. I'll settle this however you want, sweetheart."

That definitely got a reaction out of her. She looked at him like he had two heads, saying, "Are you nuts? This psycho attacked us, Tom! She stabbed you and tried to do the same to me! There's no way in hell she's getting off easy. Not if I have anything to do with it. And I will!"

God, she was magnificent in her outrage. "I always knew you were strong," he said. "You kept doubting yourself, but I knew it all along."

She didn't respond to that, but instead pursed her lips and looked toward the window. After a moment, she cleared her throat. "Anyhow, I guess her parents aren't even in the country right now so their lawyer has been handling things." She made a sound of disgust. "What loving parents, huh? They had no clue what their daughter was up to. They'd known Casey had a crush on you, but nobody thought she'd do something like this."

Beth's voice broke on her last words. She stared at the swath of bandages wrapped around his right arm, and her eyes welled up again.

He couldn't stand it anymore. Stretching past the edge of the bed, he took her hand in his unbandaged one and gave it a kiss.

"It's all right, Beth. It's not as bad as it looks."

"There was so much blood," she whispered, a single tear rolling down her cheek.

"Believe me, it was superficial. A few stitches, some ointment, some gauze. It was really nothing."

"How many stitches?"

He looked away for a brief second. "Fifty-seven."

"Fifty-seven stitches! That's not nothing, Tom!"

"I was anesthetized, Beth. The tetanus shot they gave me hurt more." He squeezed her hand. "I'll probably have a doozy of a scar, but maybe it'll make me look tougher," he said with a smile, trying to bring levity to the room.

She didn't buy it. Her solemn look traveled straight to his soul. "She could have cut a tendon, and you'd never play guitar again."

He lifted her hand for another kiss. "But she didn't, Beth. I'm all right. No long-term damage."

She pulled away and stood up, pacing to the window before turning to face him. "Why'd you risk it? Music is your whole life, and you could have lost it in an instant. Why did you risk everything?"

He didn't have to think before answering.

"Without you, I'd have nothing." His simple statement stopped her cold.

Good. Maybe now she'd really listen to him.

"C'mere. Please." He held out his hand to her. When she moved forward to take it, he pulled her down on the bed next to him. Although she settled easily against him, she plucked restlessly at the bedclothes, avoiding his eyes.

"I love music. I always have, and I always will. But if I couldn't play anymore, I'd still get by. I'd still sing, and I could always pick up another instrument. I'd find something." He lifted her chin so she had no place to look but at him. "But there is no way on earth that I could go on without you."

"But—"

"No, listen. I've heard enough of your excuses in the past few days. Now it's my turn to talk."

Beth opened her mouth to comment, but then pressed her lips together and remained quiet.

Tom said a silent word of thanks and held her tighter against him.

"You told me before that you'd hated living on the road. But you also told me it wasn't your choice." He slipped his fingers through the thick hair tumbling loose around her face. "You were a child then. Now you're a woman—the woman I want to spend the rest of my life with."

He gently pulled her closer for a brief kiss. "I'm asking you to choose that life now. With me." One more soft kiss and then Tom backed away.

Although he ached to wrap his arm around Beth, longed to feel her body against his and deepen the kiss, he knew the moment called for a cautious approach. Everything was riding on this one instant in time.

Beth stared at him, tears streaming down her face. He wanted to erase those tears more than anything. Wanted to make her happy for the rest of her life. But she had to make the decision on her own.

He waited for her answer with his heart in his throat. And, finally …

"I—"

They were both startled when the door swung open and Leo's distinct voice boomed, "Wake up, sunshine! Time to spring you before they try to shove oatmeal down your throat."

Leo came to an abrupt halt as he caught sight of Beth in Tom's arms, hastily wiping at her damp cheeks. "Oops. Forget I said anything. I'm gone."

"Nah, forget it. It's time to go anyway." Tom ignored Bethany's curious look as he nudged her off the bed. He tossed the light cotton blanket aside and shifted sideways. In short order, Leo grabbed Tom's belongings from a nearby closet and helped him change back into his clothes from the night before.

"You sure you're all right, man?" Leo asked, noticeably looking at the dried drops of blood decorating Tom's jeans. Beth had glanced at the spots, too, before quickly turning away to pick up her purse and sweater.

He kept his eyes on her as he clumsily pulled on his footwear. "Yeah, I'm fine. Just need to get back to the hotel. Gotta grab a shower and take care of some other stuff."

Beth shot him a look when he mentioned 'other stuff.' He returned it with one of his own. That's right, sweetheart. We're gonna settle this once and for all.

They needed to have absolute privacy for this discussion because he intended to employ any means necessary to get what he wanted. And there was only one answer he'd be willing to accept from her.

Yes.

Chapter Sixteen

Beth's heart thudded loudly in her chest as she followed Tom down the hotel hallway to his room.

Their room.

She had helped Leo transfer all of their belongings to this new room early this morning.

Since Roadhouse's tour had officially ended last night, the buses and equipment had to be returned to Georgia as soon as possible. Most of the band and crew members, including her father, had grudgingly headed out in the midnight hours—and only after making sure both she and Tom would be okay.

Leo, being Tom's best friend, had volunteered to remain in Albany so that Dylan and Sam's holiday plans wouldn't be disrupted.

But now Leo was gone. He'd abandoned them in favor of staying with Dylan at his family's nearby home. Beth figured Tom must've done some heavy persuading to get Leo to take off.

But then again, today had been exhausting for all of them, and Leo probably just wanted to unwind.

Forget coming back to the hotel early—circumstances had prevented it. They'd had to wait close to an hour for someone to bring Tom's discharge papers. Then they'd gone to a nearby pharmacy to pick up first-aid supplies and fill Tom's prescriptions for antibiotics and pain medicine. Computer problems caused a delay there as well.

Hunger drove them to a local pizza place around noon, and when they'd finished eating, Leo called Dylan to pick them up.

She and Tom declined Dylan's invitation to join the festivities at his parents' house, but he had insisted on dropping them at their next destination.

The police station.

With Tom being injured the night before, there'd been no time to fill out reports and give statements. Beth had assured the officers who'd showed up at the Theatre that they would come to the station today to take care of things.

So after spending yet another long afternoon in a police station answering questions and filling out paperwork, Beth should've been feeling drained. She'd barely slept last night, too worried about Tom to doze more than a couple hours at his bedside.

But right now, as she watched him insert the hotel key card and push the door open, all she felt was eager and energized. Which didn't mean a thing because she knew she had to be feeling a lot better than Tom.

She wasn't the one who'd had his arm sliced open. She wasn't the one who, judging by the lines creasing his forehead, was in severe pain. She— "Aagh!" Beth found herself yanked into the room and pressed back against the closed door.

It was just like what had happened in the Baltimore dressing room what felt like a lifetime ago.

He took her breath away.

Tom held her in place with his lean body, threading the fingers of his left hand through her hair, fanning kisses over her face, then dipping down to nuzzle her neck.

Beth's purse slid down her arm and dropped to the floor with a clunk. She couldn't move. He was single-handedly overpowering her.

Oh, who was she kidding. She was putty without him even laying a finger on her. The mere thought of him did her in.

In between hot kisses and sweet caresses, Tom murmured, "I thought I lost you. I was so scared. You can't ever leave me again, understand?"

"Yes."

That stopped him immediately. He dropped his hand and stepped away, a questioning look on his impossibly handsome face. "What exactly are you saying yes to?"

She wanted nothing more than for him to keep doing what he'd been doing—touching her, arousing her. Loving her. But she supposed it was better to get everything said. Talk first, then make love. It was a good plan.

"I'm saying yes to everything," Beth said. "I love you, Tom, and I want to marry you." She hesitated. "If you still want me, that is."

He tenderly stroked her cheek. "I'll want you forever. But are you sure?"

She hated that he had to ask that. "I wasn't sure before, about myself. I didn't know if I could handle having a real relationship with you, where I'd have to relive my childhood on the road. But now I'm okay with it."

"What changed your mind? Because I hope you're not reacting to the stress of the attack."

"It's not what happened to me, it's what happened to you." He opened his mouth to counter her words, so she hurriedly corrected herself. "I mean, what almost happened to you."

Beth reached out to spread her palm over his chest. She felt the heat of him—the heart of him—beneath his cotton shirt. And she wanted it all.

Her gaze locked with Tom's. "You could have been seriously hurt. When it first happened I didn't know the extent of your injuries, and I wanted to die. I could have lost you because of what Casey did. Then, when I found out you'd be all right, I felt even worse. And angry at myself. Because I'd been willing to throw it all away—throw us away—without even giving it a chance."

Beth leaned forward to press her trembling lips to Tom's neck. "And I have to give it a chance," she whispered.

He crushed her in his embrace, still strong despite his wound. He ravaged her mouth, and she ravaged his.

Never again would she be so idiotic. The best thing in her life was in her arms, and she had almost tossed him away like garbage.

Tom pulled back enough to say, "I have to shower before this goes any further." He gently nibbled her bottom lip. "Care to join me?"

Oh, God, she would love to. But she knew what had happened the last time they'd showered together, and it was too soon for that. No water acrobatics when he needed to recuperate.

Beth gave Tom a final kiss before turning him around and slapping his firm tush. "No, you go ahead. We'll finish this later. In bed."

He took two steps toward the bathroom before looking back, his brow cocked. "You sure?" He carefully pulled his shirt over his head while swinging his slim hips to and fro, teasing her with his sexy movements. "I can make you feel real good."

A choked laugh escaped Beth's throat. She shoved at his back, her fingers lingering just a touch too long on its broad expanse. "Go! Before I throw you down on the floor and have my way with you. Go, you stinky man!"

Her last comment stopped him cold, the grin spreading across his face now frozen in place. He lifted an arm and took a sniff. And coughed.

"Good lord, sweetheart, why didn't you tell me I reeked before you let me touch you?"

Beth smiled. "Because I love it when you touch me, smelly or not."

An expression came over his face that she'd never seen before. It was both sweet and serious. Tender and sincere.

Tom stepped forward and slid a gentle hand down her cheek as he looked deep into her eyes. "I love you, Bethany. Don't ever forget that."

"I love you, too, Tom. And I won't."

She swore his dark eyes were glistening just before he pressed his mouth to hers once again. The barest touch of his lips, the slightest tickle of his warm breath.

And then he was gone.

•

Ignoring the doctor's instructions to keep his bandages dry for forty-eight hours, Tom stepped into the warm spray and let the water run over every inch of his body. Washing up left-handed was difficult, but he somehow managed to finish in under ten minutes.

He quickly toweled off, then pulled on a loose pair of gray sweatpants and left his feet bare. He would need Beth's assistance to change the wet dressings on his arm, but after that...well, let's just say he had plans for the rest of the night.

Tom left the bathroom and saw Beth replacing the phone receiver. "Did someone call? Was it about the case?"

She turned toward him but didn't meet his gaze. "No, nobody called here. I, um, called room service to order dinner."

Tom crossed the room to her side. "My intention was to feast on you, darlin'," he murmured before leaning down to kiss her throat. A tiny red mark was all that remained of Beth's physical encounter with Casey, and once again Tom felt grateful nothing more had happened to her.

Beth's hands crept up between them, pressing warmly against his bare chest. "Tom, you need to eat." Her fingers danced lazily across his flesh, brushing lightly over his nipples and ribcage, leaving barely restrained lust in their wake. She looked up at him through her eyelashes, biting at her lower lip. "And you probably need a pain pill by now. You haven't taken one since we left the hospital."

Damn. Now that she'd mentioned it, his arm was throbbing quite a bit.

"Okay. We'll eat and I'll take a pill." She started to smile. "But don't think I'm not going to have my way with you tonight."

"Well, duh!" Beth rolled her eyes at him. "Why do you think I want you to eat? You'll need your strength for later, baby!"

They both laughed, and Tom's heart swelled with emotion. She was everything to him, and he'd cherish her always.

"Hey, if the food's not coming for a while, could you help me change these wet bandages?" He lifted his right arm and saw the humor fade from Beth's face.

"Of course! Why didn't you say something as soon as you came out? It must itch like crazy!"

Her concern for him was overwhelming, and Tom knew it wasn't borne of selfishness. Beth wanted him for himself, not for his rising musician status or what he could do for her. And that wasn't something he was used to, especially after dating Marissa.

As she unwrapped the Ace bandage and peeled off the layers of gauze, Tom watched her expression get more and more subdued. By the time his swollen, angry-looking wound was exposed to the air, her beautiful blue eyes were shimmering with unshed tears.

She gently trailed a finger alongside the dark row of tiny stitches running from the bottom of his palm to the middle of his forearm. "Oh, Tom," she whispered, then exhaled a shaky breath.

He carefully cupped the back of her head and pulled it forward, pressing a kiss to her brow before leaning his forehead against hers. "Shh, sweetheart. It's over now."

He pulled back and used his thumb to brush an escaped tear from her cheek. "Starting tonight, it's only about us. Okay? No looking back."

She straightened her shoulders and lifted her chin, a look of determination coming into her eyes. "You're right. It's over, and we have things to look forward to—like planning our wedding."

Oh, man. He'd completely forgotten she'd agreed to marry him. What a freaking idiot.

Tom shook his head and gave a self-deprecating chuckle.

"What's so funny?"

"Nothing, honey." He continued to silently berate himself. "Are you sure you know what you're getting into with me? I can be a jerk sometimes."

Beth narrowed her eyes. "I have no idea what you're thinking of, but I can definitely tell you that you were a jerk last night!"

"Last night?" Tom indicated his injured arm. "I'm a jerk because I got hurt?"

As if in pain, Beth closed her eyes and briefly pressed a hand to her temple. Then she gestured impatiently at him, glaring all the while. "No, doofus, you were a jerk because you embarrassed the hell out of me with that dedication!"

"Are you telling me my emotional plea didn't sway you in the least?" he teased.

"No! In fact, I want you despite what you did." She laid her hands on his shoulders and gave them a little shake. "Promise me you'll never do something like that again. Promise!"

"Hey, I don't need to do it again. You already gave me the answer I needed to hear." With his good hand, Tom unclamped Beth's fingers and brought her palm to his mouth for a light kiss before pressing it to the center of his chest. He kept a firm grip on her hand as he continued, "But I can't predict what's going to happen as Roadhouse gets bigger. The media can't be controlled, and our personal lives—"

"Won't be our own anymore. I know." Beth tugged her hand free and stepped closer, sliding her arms around his neck. "I can handle it, Tom. I can handle whatever I need to as long as we're together."

"Even if it means touring?"

She hesitated. "Well, actually, I've been thinking about that..."

"And?" He slid his arm around her waist, holding her tight against him. She was killing him here.

"And I was hoping to find an accounting job in Savannah. Maybe something with a temp agency so I'd have a more flexible schedule and could be with you on the road sometimes."

She dropped her gaze to stare in the vicinity of his Adam's apple. "But—and don't take this the wrong way, because I really do love you—I don't know if I want to travel with you all the time. I just..."

"Shh." He dropped a kiss on the bridge of her nose. "It's okay. You don't have to explain anything."

She looked up, eyes wide.

"Whatever makes you comfortable is fine with me. But know this, darlin'. I'll always be true to you, and you'll always be in my heart, even if we're apart for a little while. Just keep faith in me, and we'll get through whatever comes our way."

Bethany leaned into him and hugged him tight, confirming what Tom already knew: They were going to make it.

•

Beth carefully finished re-bandaging Tom's arm just in time for dinner to arrive. They spent the next hour lingering over a light meal of sandwiches and fruit, talking about the future, the past, and, ultimately, the present.

"You really have to take a pill now, Tom. I can see how uncomfortable you are." Beth stretched over the small table littered with empty dishes to trace the lines on his forehead, wishing she could take the pain away.

"I'm uncomfortable because I've had a raging hard-on for hours, and you've forced me to wait." He pulled her hand down to kiss her knuckles. "Besides, those pills make me loopy, and I want all my faculties intact so I can take care of you the right way." Tom stood and pulled her out of her seat. "Let's go, sweetheart. My patience is at its end."

Beth planted her feet. "Tell you what. You take a pain pill, and I will take care of you the right way. You just have to lie back and enjoy."

He smiled and lifted a brow. "Now there's an offer I can't refuse."

"Good. Now go take your medicine and get into bed. I'm just going to clean this mess up and put the cart outside."

Beth wanted no interruptions. Truth be told, she was probably more eager to make love than Tom was. She loved talking to him, listening to his sexy southern voice, but she wanted physical reassurance that he was all right. And what better way to affirm that than to link their hearts and bodies as one?

She pushed the room service cart into the hall, hung the 'Do not disturb' sign on the door, then closed and locked it. Beth turned to see Tom stripping out of his sweats, leaving his entire body free to be devoured by her hungry eyes.

And her lips, and her tongue …

Oh, yeah. This was going to be fun.

"I'll be out in a minute," she said, heading toward the bathroom.

"I'm not going anywhere," Tom replied as he tossed back the quilted bedcover and slid beneath the sheet. "But hurry anyway."

Beth concluded her bathroom business in what she considered to be record time. Yet when she re-entered the main room, there was no eager greeting called to her. Instead she heard only the soft sounds of even inhalations and exhalations.

He was sleeping?

Those pills apparently did more than make him loopy. They knocked him out cold.

She sighed.

Leaving only one small lamp on, Beth shed her clothes and got into the king-size bed next to Tom. He lay on his back, his injured arm near the edge of the mattress, allowing her, at the very least, to hold him as he slept.

She rested her arm on his chest, content to feel the steady beat of his heart beneath her palm. But then, of their own volition, her fingers slid over his warm skin to tangle in the wiry hairs between his nipples, and moved further down his torso to the thicker patch of hair below his navel.

Just one touch, that's all she wanted.

Beth leaned up and pushed the sheet away from Tom's lower body. He stirred restlessly but otherwise seemed unaware of her actions.

She traced a finger over his semi-erect penis, watching as it grew harder, bigger beneath her gentle caress. Then she cupped his testicles, felt their weight shifting in her palm.

He was irresistible.

She didn't necessarily want to disturb his needed sleep, but there was no way she could stop now.

One taste was all she needed. Then she'd let him be.

She scooted down so her mouth was even with his now full erection. Tucking her hair behind her ears, she leaned over to run her tongue up his shaft, one lick from base to tip.

Nope, forget it. One taste was definitely not enough.

But she somehow figured Tom would forgive her for what she was doing.

Beth moved between his legs and licked him again, a little rougher this time. He was warm and smooth in her hand.

"Mm. Oh, sweetheart." With a groan he awakened, and she felt the fingers of his uninjured hand wind though her hair, gently yet insistently guiding her head up and down in a rhythmic motion. "Yeah, just like that."

She continued the intimate stimulation, loving the sounds of appreciation that came from him when she alternated the pressure of her lips, tongue, and fingers. Intent on Tom's enjoyment, and thoroughly adding to her own as she took him closer to the edge, Beth was surprised when he pulled her away from his straining manhood.

"What—"

He pulled her up for a soft kiss. "I want you with me." He kissed her again, this time with an intensity that threatened to set her ablaze.

Moving into position above him, Beth slid down to take him inside, no barrier between them. Oh, yeah, what a way to burn.

She leaned down to press tender kisses against Tom's lips, throat, and chest. Her hips ground against his, moving faster and faster, seeking to bring them both to the place they could only find together.

Loud explosions and multicolored streaks from the capital city's nearby Fourth of July celebration turned the room into a kaleidoscope of sensations. But no sounds or light displays could distract Beth from the man on the bed beneath her, or the things he made her feel.

As a powerful climax overcame her, she let herself go, delighting in the sound of Tom's pleasure following close behind hers.

Collapsing on his chest, she made sure not to bump his wounded arm. Beth savored the feel of his strong body along hers and the light kisses he pressed to her hair, knowing one thing for sure.

Until the day she died, she'd be grateful for whatever time she spent with Tom. She loved him with all her heart, and she would deal with whatever circumstances his career brought. Whether he was in the studio or on tour, she would be there, supporting him and encouraging him. He had risked everything for her, and she'd willingly do the same for him. She would be strong for him, and for them.

Being on the road again wouldn't be hard, Beth thought as she slid to Tom's side and snuggled closer, absorbing his warmth.

Because when she was with Tom, she was home.

Lisa Lewis

Lisa Lewis lives in upstate New York with her husband, two daughters, and three cats. As a former science teacher she has always escaped reality listening to music and reading romance novels. In her first novel, Lisa has finally brought those two loves together for others to enjoy.

www.LisaLewisBooks.com